Death Leap!

Before I could get to the Leap, the cars began moving. Cody and Joe were in the second car sent around the coaster. There was an empty car half-way around the track already. I tried yelling up to the operator, but the little booth was perched too far up for them to hear me. Frank and Cody began to gain speed, flying through the first loop of the track. I could hear Cody screaming with joy. I had maybe fifteen seconds to save them. Maybe.

My eyes darted around the roller coaster, looking for some way to stop it. By the time I climbed up to the operator's booth, it would be too late. How could I stop a thousand pounds of speeding metal?

THE HARDY BOYS

Undercover Brothers®

Available from Simon & Schuster

THE **HARDY BOYS**

Undercover Brothers®

BOYS

FRANKLIN W. DIXON

#29 X-plosion

WITHDRAWN

Aladdin
New York **London** **Toronto** **Sydney**

This book is a work of fiction. Any references to historical events, real people, or real locales are used fictitiously. Other names, characters, places, and incidents are the product of the author's imagination, and any resemblance to actual events or locales or persons, living or dead, is entirely coincidental.

ALADDIN

An imprint of Simon & Schuster Children's Publishing Division
1230 Avenue of the Americas, New York, NY 10020
First Aladdin paperback edition July 2009
Text copyright © 2009 by Simon & Schuster, Inc.
All rights reserved, including the right of reproduction in whole
or in part in any form.
ALADDIN is a trademark of Simon & Schuster, Inc., and related logo is
a registered trademark of Simon & Schuster, Inc.
THE HARDY BOYS MYSTERY STORIES is a trademark of
Simon & Schuster, Inc.
HARDY BOYS UNDERCOVER BROTHERS and related logo are
registered trademarks of Simon & Schuster, Inc.
For information about special discounts for bulk purchases, please
contact Simon & Schuster Special Sales at 1-866-506-1949 or
business@simonandschuster.com.
The Simon & Schuster Speakers Bureau can bring authors to your live
event. For more information or to book an event contact the
Simon & Schuster Speakers Bureau at 1-866-248-3049 or visit our
website at www.simonspeakers.com.
Designed by Sammy Yuen Jr.
The text of this book was set in Aldine 401 BT.
Manufactured in the United States of America
10 9 8 7 6 5 4 3 2 1
Library of Congress Control Number 2009925977
ISBN 978-1-4169-7870-1
ISBN 978-1-4169-9582-1 (eBook)

TABLE OF CONTENTS

FRANK
1

In with a Bang

The crowd was still cheering, and the echo of the explosion of Mount McKenzie was fresh in my ears. *If things keep exploding at Galaxy X,* I thought, *I'm asking ATAC to issue me some earplugs.*

In fact, I had a lot to talk to ATAC about right then. We'd thought our case was over—we'd figured out who had been harassing the wealthy music producer Tyrone McKenzie and arrested them before they could ruin the opening day of his new extreme sport amusement park, Galaxy X. Tyrone loved us—well, okay, he loved me and he liked Joe. The park was awesome, with hundreds of rides, roller coasters, and games taking over the entire island. The place was crawling with celebrities, actors, and musicians. It was definitely the best mission we'd had yet.

Except for one small problem. Mount McKenzie wasn't supposed to blow up on opening day. Our only suspect, a local security guard named Wallace, was behind bars, and he couldn't have done it. And we knew it wasn't an accident, because Tyrone had received a text message on his PDA from Sk8rH8r, the nickname of the person behind the attacks on the park, right as the mountain blew up. It said I WARNED YOU! Whoever it was had threatened to ruin opening day and destroy the park. Who knew what else they had in mind besides destroying Mount McKenzie? The huge crowd of park-goers, celebrities, and press who'd lined up to get inside the gates first were now all in terrible danger. And we didn't have a clue where it was coming from. Thankfully, most of the crowd seemed to believe that the explosion was another one of Tyrone's publicity stunts.

Mount McKenzie wasn't the only thing that seemed to be exploding either. Tyrone himself was red-faced with rage. The guy's temper was legendary. Right now he looked about ready to punch somebody's lights out. But Tyrone was nothing if not a professional entertainer, and even though he wanted to kill somebody, he got up to go to the microphone and welcome everyone to the opening of Galaxy X.

I wanted to go over to Mount McKenzie and look for any evidence that might have survived the explosion, but Joe and I had been invited to sit on the welcome platform with the McKenzie family while Tyrone made his speech. Lined up next to me were Erica and Nick, Tyrone's children from his other marriages, and Delfina, Tyrone's second (or was it third?) wife, clutching the newest member of the family—Tyrone Jr. Nick was a bit of a spoiled brat, Delfina was nice but clueless, and Erica . . . well, Erica sometimes made it hard for me think around her. But in a good way. Sometimes cute girls have that effect on me. She was also really smart, and on the whole, just a great person.

At the other end of the platform I could see Joe fidgeting in his seat. He was just as desperate to get up on Mount McKenzie as I was. But Tyrone was speaking now, and with everyone's attention focused right on where we were sitting, there was no way we could slip away undetected. I sat on my hands and listened to Tyrone instead.

"Many people have asked me how I came up with the idea for Galaxy X," his voice boomed out over the loudspeaker. "And all I can tell them is that from the moment I first set eyes on this island, I knew it would one day be home to the biggest, most exciting, most advanced theme park in the world! A place where young men—and ladies— could experience *true* adventure."

The crowd went wild when he said that—hooting, screaming, stomping their feet. Tyrone had them in the palm of his hand. I had to hand it to him. He was a master at public displays.

"And," he continued, "we have one more surprise for all of you diehard fans who joined us here on opening weekend. Starting in just a few days, Cody Zane, the number-one ranked skateboarder in the world, will kick off the Cody Zane Skate or Die Competition sponsored by PowerUp energy drink. The prize for winning the competition? One lucky skater will be made into a character in the all-new Cody Zane: Skate or Die video game, which is being released next year from the fabulous folks at Sold Out Entertainment!"

If the crowd had been loud before, they were crazy now. But somewhere among all the cheering, I thought I heard a different kind of scream—one of pain and fear. And it was coming from Mount McKenzie. Someone might have been up there!

Before I could do anything, Tyrone gave the signal, and the gates to the park slowly parted. People were running everywhere. The speakers began blasting music and nearly drowned out the noise of the crowd with Mr. Nice Guyz' biggest hit, "(No More) Mr. Nice Guyz." No one else seemed to have noticed anything. Maybe I'd hallucinated the scream.

Then I saw it. There was an arm sticking out of the rubble on top of Mount McKenzie! Someone *had* been up there during the explosion. Whoever it was would need serious medical attention.

Now no one was paying attention to us anymore. The crowd was rushing the park, Tyrone was screaming into his cell phone (as usual), and the rest of the family had wandered off. I raced over to where Joe was.

"There's someone up there!" I screamed to be heard over the noise of the crowd, pointing to Mount McKenzie.

"What?"

I tried again, but it was no use over the noise. Finally I just spun Joe around and pointed to the arm poking through the rocks. Joe raced to the edge of the platform and jumped down, right into the sea of running, shoving, screaming people. It was like trying to swim against the tide—a tide made up of flying elbows and kicking feet. Everyone wanted to be the first one on the rides. Joe and I managed to make it halfway to Mount McKenzie, but then someone kicked me in the back of the knee. Before I knew what had happened, I was on the ground.

Around me, dozens of pairs of legs were trampling up and down. I tried to get up, but there was no room. I got stepped on again and again. And no one even seemed to notice I was under them! In a few seconds I was going to be crushed to death by an army of distracted teenagers!

Suddenly an arm shot down out of the crowd and pulled me up.

"You okay?" Joe yelled.

I nodded, too out of breath to answer him. Even without trying to, we were moving closer to our destination, pushed along by the wild, surging tide of people. All we had to do was keep our balance and we'd get there eventually. After a few more minutes of pushing, we were able to grab hold of the sides of the remains of Mount McKenzie and start climbing.

The mountain was still incredibly hot. The explosion had blown away the layer of dirt and grass that Tyrone's gardeners had built on the outside of the mountain, exposing the metal framework at its interior. We could use that as scaffolding to climb up, like a giant jungle gym. A spiky, hot jungle gym.

"Ow!" Joe screamed, and pulled his hand back from the piece of metal he'd been about to use as a handhold. "Watch out," he said. "It's still hot from the explosion."

There were jagged pieces of metal everywhere— some hot, some sharp. It was like an obstacle course, only deadly. Twice I nearly impaled myself on pieces of metal I didn't see until the last moment. We had to climb at an angle, slowly making our away around the mountain even as we went upward, like a giant spiral. Finally, however, we reached the top—or at least what remained of it.

From here you could see the entire park. The crowd seemed like an army of ants, spreading out from the gates at the entrance and slowly over-whelming every ride and attraction that was open. I could hear a weak groaning noise coming from somewhere underneath the rubble. Then I spot-ted the arm I had seen before—covered in dirt and nearly invisible now that it was no longer moving. I hoped we weren't too late.

"Over here," I called to Joe. Together we moved some of the larger pieces of debris and dug our way down.

"Be careful!" came the muffled shout from the person below. Apparently, we were in time.

"This jacket cost four thousand dollars! If you tear it, I swear I'll sue you."

Something about that voice—and that attitude—sounded familiar. Joe and I lifted up a few more pieces of rock to reveal Bret Johnston, the lead singer of Mr. Nice Guyz. What was he doing on top of Mount McKenzie? Could he have been behind the explosion, and somehow gotten caught in his own blast? Or was he just an innocent (if irritating) bystander?

Bret certainly didn't seem happy to see Joe and me.

"I said, be careful you . . . monkeys!"

"Do you want us to leave you under there?" Joe asked. When Bret didn't answer, Joe threw his hands in the air and pretended to walk away.

"Hey! Where are you going? Wait! Stop! Help me!" Bret started screaming again. With a shrug, Joe returned, and we dug him the rest of the way out. Aside from a few scratches and bruises, he didn't seem to be hurt—pretty suspicious for someone just caught in a huge explosion. Maybe he'd buried himself on purpose. . . .

"What were you doing up here?" I asked.

Bret was brushing dirt off his clothes and seemed shocked to find we were still there, bothering him.

"I don't see what business it is of yours. But if you must know, I was planning on skiing down the mountain when my song came on—as a special reward for all my fans who had come to see me. The next thing I knew, the ground was flying out from underneath me."

Bret seemed to think today was all about him, and that Mount McKenzie exploding was a personal attack. I got the feeling he thought that way about everything. Still, it was pretty strange that he was up here alone when the mountain exploded. We needed to get him to a hospital and make sure he was okay. But after that, I wanted to look into his story a little more.

Suspect Profile

Name: Bret Johnston

Hometown: Corpus Christi, Texas

Physical description: Brown hair, blue eyes, 6'1", 180 lbs, age 17. According to his fan sites, "drop dead-gorgeous." Maybe it should be "drop-DEADLY gorgeous."

Occupation: Lead singer of Mr. Nice Guyz

<u>Background</u>: Originally from southern Florida, but he now considers himself a "citizen of the world."

<u>Suspected of</u>: Blowing up Mount McKenzie, and possibly sabotaging the other opening day celebrations at Galaxy-X.

<u>Possible motive</u>: He can't stand to have the spotlight taken off of him for one moment. What better way to get attention then by faking an injury?

<u>Suspicious behavior</u>: Why was he on Mount McKenzie when it exploded? He was supposed to be down at the opening celebration. And he certainly seems self-centered enough to blow up Mount McKenzie if there was any way he could benefit from it.

The Other Mount McKenzie Explodes

"How dare they!" Tyrone screamed at the top of his lungs. When he really let go, he didn't need a microphone to be heard. I'd seen him in some bad moods over the course of our case, but nothing like this before. He was stomping up and down his office, slamming doors, and throwing things. He was like a two-year-old. A *giant* two-year-old. He'd been like this ever since Frank and I had gotten back from taking Bret Johnston to the hospital. Bret had said he was fine, and I would have been more than happy to leave him on top of Mount McKenzie, but Frank insisted we take him to get checked out. At least this way, we knew where he was if we needed to question him.

"Mount McKenzie was the centerpiece of my park! Someone is going to pay for this. I'll wring their necks!" Even if he was going overboard about it, I understood why Tyrone was so angry. Someone had got him good when they blew up Mount McKenzie—and we had no idea who it could be. Yet. If we could just get out of Tyrone's office and start investigating the explosion, however, I had no doubt we could clear this up pretty quickly. Hopefully, with enough time to get to explore the park, too. And maybe take part in the Cody Zane Skate or Die Competition . . .

Frank must have had the same idea, because he tried to interrupt Tyrone's yelling to say something. Tyrone turned on him.

"And you! I don't want to hear it. What good are you, anyway? Fancy ATAC and all your supposed detective brilliance—and you couldn't even stop someone from blowing up a mountain! It's huge! How could you screw this up?"

"Well," Frank said, "we had a suspect in custody, Tyrone. And he'd admitted to causing the other destruction—"

"Bah! I don't want to hear it. Clearly you didn't catch the right person, or else the mountain wouldn't have BLOWN UP! Or are you trying to tell me that was an accident?" Tyrone seemed to be enjoying himself now, like he had an audience. From what I could tell, he seemed to like yelling at people. Nick was smirking in the background, taking great pleasure in our fall from Tyrone's good graces.

"And your 'suspect in custody,' Wallace? He doesn't even know what text messages are. He's clearly not 'Skater Hater,' or whatever this freak is calling himself."

It looked like Tyrone was about to explode. His face was bright red, and there was one big vein on his forehead that throbbed with every word he said. Or screamed, as it were. Nick was standing behind him, trying to cover up his laughter. He seemed to be pleased to watch Tyrone yelling at someone else for a change. I had to admit, it was kind of funny to watch Frank fall from being Tyrone's golden boy. Me, I was just standing out of the way and trying not to get any of Tyrone's spit on me. He was so angry, he was nearly foaming at the mouth.

"But Tyrone, he—," Frank tried again. *Big* mistake.

"Don't you call me Tyrone! It's Mr. McKenzie to you!"

"Give it a rest, *Tyrone*." Erica's voice came from behind Tyrone's desk, where she'd made herself comfortable. She was sitting on his chair, feet up on the desk. It was pretty obvious that Erica didn't get along with Tyrone. She was his stepdaughter, and they seemed to fight a lot. "It's not Frank's fault that people don't like you."

Erica was supercute, and smart, too—and she totally had a crush on Frank, which is probably why she was sticking up for him. Erica talking back to Tyrone totally made Frank blush. He's not that smooth with the ladies (unlike me). It made Tyrone go red in the face too—but for different reasons.

"Don't you get started with me, Erica. I am your father and you will address me as such. Now go help your mother with Tyrone Junior."

That touched a nerve.

"She's not my mother!" Erica yelled back. She kicked her feet across the desk, spilling Tyrone's papers everywhere. Then she ran out of the office. Looked like she had inherited some of her step-dad's temper. I couldn't see her face very well, but I was pretty sure she was crying. Nick was laughing out loud by this point, and Tyrone yelled for him to get out of the office as well. They certainly seemed like one big happy family. Not.

"As for the two of you," Tyrone said, pointing at Frank and me, "nothing had better happen during the Cody Zane Skate or Die Competition, you hear me? I have a lot of money riding on this. If you can't handle it, I'll hire some people who can."

Tyrone pulled his PDA out of his pocket and threw it at Frank, who caught it right before it hit him in the face.

"Now take this and figure out who this Skater Hater is. I want results, not more excuses! Go on, get out!"

He didn't need to tell me twice. I was out of that office before you could count to three.

"So, where to now?" I asked Frank.

I could still hear Tyrone screaming inside his office, even though we'd left the building. He didn't seem like the kind of guy who got over things quickly. Thankfully, his office was in the part of the park that was off-limits to visitors, so no one except his family, Frank, and me had to hear him.

Lucky us.

"Well, Bret Johnston should be out of the hospital by now. Maybe we should go talk to him some more?" Frank suggested.

"Ugh. The last thing I want to do is talk to him. He's such a spoiled brat. Besides, I don't really think he had anything to do with the explosion. He's such an attention hog—I believe him when he says he was planning on skiing down the mountain to his song to impress his fans."

"Yeah," Frank agreed. "It doesn't make much sense for him to have blown up Mount McKenzie. But right now, he's our only suspect. And he *was* around when most of the other 'accidents' happened, so who knows? I'll ask ATAC to dig up any information they can find on him."

"You know what we need to do? One of us needs to enter the Skate or Die Competition. To keep an eye on things from the inside."

Frank quirked his eyebrow at me.

"To keep an eye on things? Or because you're obsessed with Cody Zane?"

"I'm not obsessed with Cody Zane! I'm just pretty sure we could be friends, if we ever met in real life. He seems like a cool guy. And I didn't say *I* had to be the one to enter the competition. It could be you. But I've been practicing, and I could totally win it."

Frank sighed and shook his head.

"Come on," he said. "You can enter the competition tomorrow. But for now, let's go back up to Mount McKenzie and see if whoever did this left behind any clues."

Frank started walking back toward the park, when all of a sudden his pocket started buzzing.

"ATAC?" I asked him.

"No," he said, reaching into his pocket. "It's Tyrone's PDA."

We both stared at it for a moment as it vibrated in Frank's hand. Then I took it and flipped it open. I figured he'd given it to us—well, okay, *thrown* it at us—so he meant for us to look at it. And even if he didn't, what he didn't know wouldn't hurt him.

The screen blinked with an incoming message from someone named 4Real. I clicked on it.

SK8 OR DIE? HOW ABOUT SK8 AND DIE? the screen read.

"Uh-oh," I said. "Looks like Skater Hater has found a friend."

FRANK

3

Living on the Edge

"Well, guess that changes our plans," Joe said, staring at the message on Tyrone's PDA device.

"What do you mean?" I asked.

"Isn't it obvious? We've got to go find Cody Zane right now and warn him. He's clearly in danger."

"I'm sure he's got bodyguards with him. Besides, who knows if this is directed at him, or just more threats at the park itself?" We needed to be ATAC agents, not fan boys. But there was no telling that to Joe. He just kept insisting that we needed to go make sure Cody was all right.

Tyrone's PDA started buzzing again. Joe opened up the new message.

CODY ZANE & ALL THOSE OTHER SELLOUTS
BETTER WATCH OUT!!

4Real, it seemed, was a poet.

"Okay, fine," I said. "We'll go talk to Cody."

"Yes!" Joe jumped up in the air and pumped his fist.

"You're going to be like this the entire time we work on this case, aren't you?" I asked.

"Yep. Probably." Joe skipped a few steps and pounded his fist in the air again. He was going to drive me crazy.

The whole way over to the VIP section of the park, Tyrone's PDA kept going off with new threats from 4Real. They were all against Cody, the competition, and "sellouts," "fakes," and "phonies." Whoever he was, 4Real definitely had a lot of anger issues. Tyrone was going to explode (again!) when he heard about this.

The VIP section of Galaxy X was an area of luxurious private cabins just for celebrities. It was like a separate island in the middle of the park, with a moat surrounding it and only one way in, a long bridge made entirely out of clear plastic, so it looked like you were walking on air. It had all sorts of special attractions that were off-limits to ordinary park visitors. There was a restaurant that delivered around the clock and would fry anything—from chicken to candy bars. The water fountains all had buttons on them to choose among water, soda, lemonade, and iced tea. When it rained, a giant dome rose up to cover the entire area. To make the celebrities happy, Tyrone guaranteed that no reporters were allowed in the VIP area. There were also a number of rides and games that were open only to VIPs—a private pool, bumper cars with specially made luxury-brand cars, even a helicopter pad for celebrities wanting to avoid the rest of the park entirely. When Tyrone said something was exclusive, he meant it.

We found Cody chilling by the VIP skate ramp with his whole entourage—photographers, bodyguards, and a host of skaters that made up the "Zaniacs," his handpicked and trained skate team. The ramp itself was surrounded by palm trees, with hammocks strung in between them. There was even a hot tub hidden in the shade, where Cody, his girlfriend (the famous model/skater London), and his best friend and fellow skater David Sanders were all stretched out. Together, the three of them were the judges for the Skate or Die Competition. Even wet, Cody's pitch-black hair managed to stick straight up in his infamous "porcupine" hairdo. In person, London was even more beautiful than she was in all the photos I'd seen. And David . . . David just looked like a normal guy. Right now, like a normal guy who was half-asleep in a hot tub.

For all the skateboarders hanging out, no one seemed to have used the ramp yet. Everyone was sitting around, updating their blogs and surfing the web on little handheld computers, or posing for pictures, or just relaxing.

Joe and I headed directly over to the hot tub, but Cody's bodyguards stopped us before we got within fifteen feet. Two of them, dressed in matching gray suits and dark sunglasses, stood directly in our path.

"Can we help you?" one of them asked. He was so tall, I was staring directly at the breast pocket of his suit. I couldn't believe he was wearing a suit in this weather. They must have been really hot, but neither one of them looked like they were sweating or uncomfortable. In fact, for all the emotion they showed, they could have been carved from stone.

"Hi. I'm Frank Hardy, and this is my brother, Joe. We need to talk to Cody."

"I'm afraid Mr. Zane isn't available at the moment," the guard said in a firm voice.

"What? But he's right over there. I can see him!"

"Hey, guys," Cody's voice rang out from the hot tub. "It's cool. They're those secret agent guys. Let 'em come over."

Well, that ruined any cover we might have had. I nearly had to run to keep up with Joe, who was so excited I'd swear he was *skipping* over to the hot tub.

"Hi, Cody," Joe said. For once, it wasn't the hot girl who had his total attention. In fact, he barely seemed to notice that London and David were there.

"Hey, guys, come on in! The water's great." Cody splashed his arm in the water, sending a hot wave flowing over the edge. London shrieked. David cracked his eyes open and then seemed to fall right back to sleep.

"I wish we could, my man. But we're here on business."

My man? Who was Joe trying to kid?

"That's cool. I hear that. I know how you secret agent types need to roll. So what's the what?"

"We've been getting some threats against you and the competition," I broke in on their bro fest.

"That's cool, man," Cody said. "I mean, not cool at all. But cool. You know what I mean?"

Cody didn't seem particularly concerned. I was going to have to make it clearer to him that this was a big deal.

"Death threats, even. And there have been other strange things happening around the park. We think you might be in danger."

"Death threats!" yelled London. "Awesome! They're totally a sign that you've made it. I remember my first death threats, when I was on the cover of *Vague* two years ago. You're in the big leagues now, baby." She hugged him, and Cody laughed.

"Whoa, crazy," he said. "Death threats."

"I got death threats in Japan during this competition I was just in." David had opened his eyes again. "I'm kind of a big deal in Asia. In fact—"

"Don't worry, Cody," Joe cut David off. "I'm entering the Skate or Die Competition to make sure nothing happens."

"Right on," said Cody. He stretched out his hand, and he and Joe bumped fists. "Let's see what you've got, man."

Cody snapped his fingers, and one of the Zaniacs came running over holding a board and a helmet. He handed them to Joe.

"These, my friend, are a top-of-the-line Hubris skateboard and helmet," Cody said. "Each board is handmade out of a special premium alloy blend invented by scientists at NASA. With Hubris, you feel like you'll never fall. It's got the Cody Zane seal of approval, so skate hard."

I nearly laughed. Cody sounded like he was reading off of a script. Joe was totally hypnotized, though. He buckled the helmet around his head while Cody and London got out of the hot tub and toweled off. David stayed behind. He huffed and rolled his eyes while Cody was talking, and then seemed to drift off back to sleep.

We all walked over to the ramp. Cody, London, and I took seats on the special luxury recliners that were built around it, while Joe got ready to skate. Each recliner had a lever that could raise it up in the air, so that no one had a bad seat or a blocked view. Inside the arms of the recliners were little inset fridges filled with drinks and snacks. There was a pile of knee pads and elbow guards next to the ramp, and Joe put on a pair of each. He looked like he was in heaven.

It didn't look like we were going to learn anything here, and Cody's bodyguards seemed to have everything pretty well in hand. I figured I'd watch Joe skate and then see if I could learn anything more about the explosion at Mount McKenzie or the other protesters that Wallace had been involved with. Joe could stay behind and play with Cody, but I wanted to find some answers. The competition started tomorrow, and we were still grasping at straws.

Joe started out slowly, kicking off and heading up one side of the ramp and back down. After a few passes, he started to gain some real speed. He wasn't kidding—he had been practicing. He started catching some air on each side, rising up above the lip of the ramp on every pass and then landing back on it. Finally, on his fifth pass, he got to the edge of the ramp and reached down to grab it and perform his first trick.

Suddenly Joe screamed with pain. He rolled down the ramp in a ball, his board tumbling after him. Behind him was a thin trail of blood!

JOE

4

Shredded

My hands felt like they were burning, and
my head was ringing from hitting the hard
plastic of the ramp on my way down. I had
no idea what had happened, except that as soon as
I touched the ramp, my hands exploded in pain.
Thanks to my ATAC training, I was able to pull
away as soon as I realized something was wrong;
otherwise I could have been seriously injured by
whatever was up there.

I heard people running and a sound like a tropical
bird, somewhere between a scream and a laugh. It
had to be London making that noise. I couldn't let
her, or any of the other Zaniacs, near the skate ramp—
who knows what other dangers it might hold?

"I'm all right!" I yelled out. "But nobody touch the ramp!"

I didn't want anyone else to get hurt, and until Frank and I had a chance to figure out what had happened, everyone needed to stay back. I got to my feet and looked at my hands. Two straight cuts went down the palms of each, as though I had grabbed a knife by the blade instead of the handle.

"What happened?" Frank was standing in front of me. Wordlessly I showed him my hands. Frank pulled a bottle of water out of his bag and poured it over my cuts to clean them. Then he pulled off his shirt and tore it into strips, which he tied into bandages around my cuts. It would keep them clean until I had a chance to have them looked at. Thankfully, I'd pulled away quickly enough that the cuts were shallow, and already the blood flow was beginning to slow.

London laughed again and whistled at Frank, who was now shirtless. I just don't get it—even when I'm the one who's hurt, all the girls go for Frank. They must all be into that shy, blushing, TOTAL NERD type.

"You all right, man?" Cody clapped me on the shoulder. He tossed a "Zaniac!" T-shirt in Frank's direction, and Frank hurried to get dressed again.

"Yeah," I told Cody. "This is nothing—you

should see some of the injuries I've gotten in other investigations." Right now, I couldn't think of one that had ever hurt worse than this, but I'm sure there'd been others. Probably.

Frank rolled his eyes at me. "Come on, let's see what happened."

The back of the ramp had a set of stairs leading up to the platform at the top. We climbed up and looked at the edge. Someone had installed a thin strip of razor-sharp metal across the lip of the ramp on both sides. If someone had put their entire weight down on it, they could have been seriously injured, maybe even lost a finger. For a professional skater like Cody, it could have spelled the end of his career. Looked like 4Real wasn't kidding!

Carefully Frank and I pulled the metal strips off and put them in our bags to check for fingerprints later. Already my hands had stopped bleeding, and the pain was lessening.

Cody's bodyguards were on high alert and had fanned out in a circle around the skate ramp, looking for trouble. Whoever had done this was probably long gone, though. That was why Cody needed an ATAC agent with him at all times—someone who could think through danger and really protect him. Like me. Certainly his friends weren't going to do it. None of the Zaniacs seemed all that concerned. London found the whole thing hysterical. She couldn't stop laughing the same high-pitched shriek of a laugh. And David hadn't even gotten out of the hot tub yet.

"Whoa," Cody said when I showed him the metal strips.

"This is the sort of thing we're here to watch for," I assured him.

"Great, 'cause like . . . somebody could have gotten seriously hurt!"

"Nah," said David, who had finally woken up and joined everyone else. "It's probably just some stupid prank. Or else some unfinished piece of construction."

"Yeah." Cody laughed, sounding relieved. "You're totally right."

He was still a little freaked out, but since no one else seemed to think it was a big deal, he shook it off. Together, Cody, London, and David all headed back to the hammocks, already bored by the whole business of my near-death experience.

"None of them seem worried at all," Frank whispered to me.

"I know. All the more reason I need to be in the Skate or Die Competition, right?"

"What about your hands? You can't skate with those."

"They're just scratches. I'll be fine."

Frank looked at me skeptically and poked my palm.

"Ow!" I yelled. "Okay, so they're a little more than scratches. But we need someone in that competition, and you don't know how to skate."

"I like that attitude, man." Without either of us noticing, Cody had drifted back over. "Spoken like a true Zaniac. Why don't you stick around? I think we're all going to do some practice skates later. You can join us. Get you ready for tomorrow's competition."

Cody Zane had just invited me to hang out with him. This was officially our best mission ever. Now there was no way I was backing out of the competition. And once I won, I'd have to hang out with Cody while they made the video game, of course. And after that, maybe he'd want to join ATAC.

In the back of my mind, I started to notice a strange noise. It was a long way off, but it sounded like a crowd of people shouting. Or laughing? I couldn't make it out. Frank clearly heard it as well—his ears were perked up and his head cocked as he tried to make out what it could be.

Suddenly a number of the park security guards went sprinting by, over the bridge and out of the

VIP section. Frank and I scrambled up onto the ramp and looked out over the park. Crowds of people were running through the public area, all headed toward the entrance. There seemed to be some sort of riot going on.

"We've got to get over there," said Frank. "It looks like just what we need—more trouble."

"Right—you'd better get over there," I said to him.

"Me? What about you?"

"One of us has to stay here and protect Cody, of course. What if this is all just a diversion to get at him?"

Frank snorted and pointed at Cody's bodyguards. "I think he's got all the protection he needs, Joe."

"They wouldn't have saved him from slicing his hands open on the ramp. He needs me here."

"Fine. Stay here. I'm going to go and find out what's happening. I'll give you a ring if I solve the case without you."

Frank took off at a run. He was just jealous that Cody liked me better. Speaking of which, I needed to stick to him like glue. So if he was going to skate, I had to get ready to skate too.

The life of an ATAC agent is tough sometimes. . . .

Punk'd!

The closer I got to the park entrances, the louder everything got. And the more crowded. There was definitely some screaming going on, but also laughing. Lots of laughing. If it was a riot, it was unlike any I had ever seen before. I couldn't believe Joe had stayed behind with Cody—but I guess he did have a point. This could have all been a plot to get him alone and unguarded.

I felt a buzzing in my pocket, but this time it was my phone. Without even looking, I knew it had to be Tyrone. I braced myself, then answered.

"Where are you two? What do you think I'm paying you for?" He was screaming so loudly that I had no trouble hearing him over the noise of the crowd. In fact, I had to hold the phone a good six inches away from my ear.

"Tyrone—I mean, Mr. McKenzie, you're not paying us. We work for ATAC, and—"

"And I don't care who you work for! Just get your lazy butts down to the front gate and deal with this situation pronto. Do you understand?"

Tyrone hung up before I could say anything. He was going to give himself a heart attack if he kept up like this. It couldn't be good for his blood pressure. And how could he scream so much and never lose his voice?

I wish he hadn't hung up without telling me what was going on. I'd seen two more groups of guards scurrying toward the gate. Whatever was happening, Tyrone must have called every security person in the place. I couldn't help but wonder if this was a set-up. Maybe it was a good thing that Joe had stayed behind with Cody.

I was winded by the time I got to the entrance of the park. I paused, hands on knees, trying to catch my breath as I took in the scene before me. It was utter chaos. Most everyone was standing around in a big circle, but some people were running and screaming. Others were just pointing and laughing. No one seemed to know what to make of what was happening.

A group of skateboarders seemed to be causing most of the trouble. They were flying around the plaza, chasing people, doing tricks, whooping and yelling. There seemed to be a ton of them—everywhere I looked, one of them was chasing someone around the square, or being chased by the security guards, or both at the same time. It seemed like a giant game.

But if the skateboarders were playing, the security guards weren't. The guards were getting angrier and angrier as the skaters dodged and weaved around them. More than one was red in the face and sitting on the ground, exhausted.

As I watched, one of the guards who was still on his feet lunged at a skater who had been taunting him by riding closer and closer. The skater jumped and the guard went flying through the air, landing on his stomach. Laughing, the skater landed on his board and took off rolling.

The skater nearest me kept switching from riding her board normally to riding it while doing a handstand. The crowd around was laughing and applauding. Another skater was riding her board popped up so she was just on the back wheels, like a cyclist doing a wheelie. Somehow she managed to go up on just *one* wheel. These were some of the most amazing skaters I'd ever seen. If it weren't for the security guards—and Tyrone's angry phone call—I would have guessed that they were some sort of promotional demonstration for the Skate or Die Competition.

I tried to count the skateboarders, but they were moving so fast it was nearly impossible. If I had to guess, I would have said there were about fifteen of them, but I wasn't sure. It didn't help that they were dressed in all black, making it hard to keep them separate. They made up for it with their hair and faces, however—I saw bright green Mohawks and long purple dreadlocks; earrings, nose rings, and lip rings. One boy had elaborate face paint on that made him look like a tiger. At least, I hoped it was face paint.

Behind the skateboarders, at the entrance to the park, was what looked to be . . . a marching band? But not like any marching band I'd ever seen before. There were no school uniforms here. The band members had on crazy outfits, all black and bright green, with glitter and stripes everywhere. The tuba said RUDE on it in big letters. The snare drum player had bright pink hair. The trombones seemed to have created a limbo line, and some of the skaters were flying underneath and doing tricks. With them was a crazy group of dancers and acrobats. The band and dancers seemed to be supporting the skaters, playing music for them to dance to. All of a sudden, at a break in the song they were playing, the band waved their instruments in the air and began to chant, "Uh-oh, this park has got to go!"

That's when I saw the banner hanging from the entrance to the park. GALAXY X IS A FAKE! it read. It looked like the skaters weren't here to take part in the competition. . . .

I had no idea what Tyrone expected me to do. I doubted I'd have better luck than the guards at catching any of these guys. They were far too fast. And they seemed to be enjoying the chase, so it wouldn't even be a hassle if I joined in. Besides, the skaters weren't hurting anyone, just causing a big spectacle. They were also blocking the entrance to the park, I realized. And if everyone was here watching them, that meant no one was out buying things or spending money on the rides. No wonder Tyrone was so upset!

The skaters also seemed to be tossing things in the air, but I couldn't make out what they were. Pieces of paper, it looked like. Or maybe confetti? It was hard to tell at a distance.

"I don't like skateboarding much, but this is hysterical."

I was so caught up in watching the skaters, I

hadn't noticed that Erica had crept up beside me. She was grinning from ear to ear, as if this were the funniest thing she'd seen in years.

"You're right," I said. "This is pretty funny."

In fact, it was almost like watching the Three Stooges, or some other old slapstick comedy. For the next fifteen minutes, the guards kept chasing the skaters, and the skaters just kept making fools out of them. Aside from the few people who tried to walk across the plaza and got caught up in the show, everyone seemed to be having a great time. The band kept playing, and soon the whole crowd was dancing and having fun.

That is, until Tyrone showed up with all the remaining security guards. His yelling could be heard over the noise of the crowd, and the smiles slipped away from people's faces as they realized this wasn't part of the Galaxy X experience.

"Typical," said Erica. "Leave it to Tyrone to ruin everyone's fun."

Tyrone screamed a bunch of commands at the guards, and they formed a giant ring around the plaza. That seemed to be the cue for the band to exit, and they backed out of the park playing a sad, slow song. The guards started walking forward carefully, enclosing the remaining skaters in a ring. Right before they were completely trapped, some hidden signal most have gone out among them. All the skaters turned as one and shot directly at the gate, barely inching through the gaps between the guards. In just a few seconds, they were all gone. The crowd booed at the guards.

On their way to the exit, one of the skaters shot right past me. As he did, he tossed a piece of paper in my direction. As the chaos calmed down and people began to head back in to the park, I reached down to pick it up.

On it, a crudely drawn Galaxy X logo had been crossed out with big slashes. Below it was a rant against the park.

"We will shut this park down! Real skaters don't need to pay fifty dollars a day to skate. . . ."

It went on from there, a full-page attack on Galaxy X and Tyrone McKenzie. The skaters accused Tyrone of tearing down the skate ramps they had built by hand and taking the land away from them—only to charge them money to come back. They promised that they would shut down the park and the "fakes" who ran it. At the end were the words "Skater culture not for sale," which sounded exactly like something 4Real would say.

Suddenly, the whole thing seemed a lot less funny.

May the Best Man Lose

"I think I've got it figured out." It was the opening morning of the Skate or Die Competition, and all around Frank and me, the crowd was going wild. However many people had been in the park yesterday, there were easily double that number today. It was a mob scene. A giant stadium full of screaming fans surrounding ten beautiful, state-of-the-art, competition-size skate ramps. Each one was a different color and had a unique mural spray painted on it by a different famous graffiti artist. Tyrone sure knew how to go all out.

"Oh yeah?" said Frank, focusing his attention on me. "So what is it?"

"It's simple. I need to start with something big—

something that will really get the judges' attention. Everyone else is going to start off slow, work their way up. I'm going to blow this thing up from the very beginning, so Cody knows I mean business."

I'd been thinking about it all night, and I could already see myself on the winning stand, with Cody next to me. It was going to be a piece of cake.

"Oh," said Frank. "And here I thought you might be talking about our case. You know, the mission we've been sent on? By ATAC? Maybe you could remember that at all?" He threw his hands up in the air and stalked off in to the crowd.

Whatever, I thought. Frank was just jealous because he was in the doghouse with Tyrone, and Cody and I were clearly on our way to being best buds. Envy was such an ugly emotion, but I'd forgive him, because today was going to be *awesome*.

Besides, we'd been up since before dawn making sure that everything was safe for the competition, so he didn't have to act like I had forgotten our mission. We'd searched each of the ramps and the stage. We'd found nothing—no traps, no bombs, not even a threatening Post-it note. Tyrone had had his guards surrounding the stadium all night long, and they guaranteed that no one had gotten in or out. There were metal detectors at each of the entrances. He was taking no chances this time.

But I didn't have time to think about all of that right now. The competition was about to start, and I needed to get in the zone. The opening day was a simple round robin. The hundred or so contestants would be paired up randomly, and ten pairs would skate at a time. Each person would have five passes to show off their stuff, and then the judges would decide who moved on to the next round. Cody wasn't even a judge for the first few rounds. Only twenty-five people would move on to the second day of competition, and I was ready to be one of them!

And while I was kicking butt, Frank would be up in the stands watching Cody closely, to make sure no one tried anything. It was a less fun job, but someone had to do it—and I was glad it wasn't me. Frank would be watching Cody. Cody would be watching me.

Tyrone had constructed a special platform for the judging table. It stood at the center of the arena, surrounded by the different skate ramps. Cody, London, David, and Tyrone were all up there now. Behind the long judges' table hung Cody's first-ever skateboard, which he had built by hand. It was legendary in the skating world. He no longer skated on it, but he was known to bring it everywhere he went for good luck.

Cody stood up and started to walk to the podium at the center of the stage. The crowd grew quiet as he began to speak.

"Welcome to the first annual Cody Zane Skate or Die Competition!" Cody yelled over the microphone. The mass of assembled contestants exploded in screams. Everyone was ready to get out there and show off.

"I hope you've all come ready to show me your stuff today, because only one person will be starring in my new Cody Zane video game with me. And it could be you. If you're good enough."

It's going to be me, I thought. *It has to be.*

"We all have things we like to do before a big competition. Some people have lucky charms or special rituals. Me? I drink PowerUp, the only energy drink fortified with a full day's worth of vitamins, minerals, and caffeine."

Cody opened a can and proceeded to drink the entire thing in one long gulp.

"Ahhh," he said. "Delicious. I also like to make sure that I've got on my lucky Kickflip brand shoes, specifically designed for the World Skating Team Championship."

Cody went on and on about the different products and clothes he used to "be the best I can be." He sounded like an infomercial. Finally, after ten more minutes of product placement, he made the announcement everyone had been waiting for.

"The first pairings are being set up now, and the competition will begin in ten minutes. Remember—skate hard!"

Finally! I thought it was never going to start. I started stretching and getting ready. One of the organizers came up to me with a clipboard.

"Joe Hardy?" he asked.

"That's me!"

"You'll be skating against Lenni Wolff in the first round, on the purple ramp. Good luck."

Frank was about to take off for the stands when Erica came up to us. She looked worried.

"Hey, Frank, hey, Joe. Good luck today."

"Thanks," I said. "I'm surprised you're here. I thought you didn't like skating."

"I don't, really," she said. "It's just . . ."

"What?" asked Frank.

"I heard that Bret Johnston was your main suspect. Is it true?"

I wondered where she had heard that. Given the way her stepfather yelled, it had probably been impossible for her *not* to hear it. Frank hesitated for a moment, then answered her.

"Well, he's definitely a suspect. But we don't have a lot of information right now. Why?"

Erica looked torn for a moment. She looked around, then leaned in and dropped her voice to a whisper.

"Well," she said, "I thought he was just hitting on me, you know? But every time he gets me alone, all he talks about is the park, and Tyrone, and what the plans are for the skating competition."

"Thanks for letting us know," I said. It wasn't anything particularly suspicious, but it was nice of Erica to tell us. I started to walk toward the ramp, but she wasn't finished.

"That's not it. The night before the park opened, I heard him complaining about how Cody Zane is getting so much more money and publicity for doing this, and how Cody is nowhere near as big a star as he is. He sounded pretty angry about it."

Frank looked at me, and I knew what he was thinking. Jealousy and money were two pretty good motives for murder. I was about to ask Erica some more questions, when an announcement came over the loudspeaker for the first round of the competition.

"I've got to get to my ramp," I said.

"Ugh," said Erica. "I'm going to go before the skating starts. I just wanted to let you guys know. I don't think he could have done anything, but . . ."

"Thanks," said Frank. "I'm going to be watching from the stands. I could walk you back that way, if you'd like."

If I didn't know any better, I'd say my brother was trying to be smooth!

As Erica and Frank walked away from the skating area, I hurried out to the ramp and got my helmet and pads on. Cody had offered to let me borrow some of his gear, but that seemed like an unfair advantage, so I brought my own. Lenni was already there, sprawled out on the ground with his helmet on. He was short and on the skinny side, dressed in all black.

Piece of cake, I thought.

I was up first. I leaped up in the air as they called my name, and the crowd cheered. I turned toward the stage and was certain that Cody was watching me. Or at least kind of looking in my direction. Maybe.

I had decided to put my most difficult trick first. I was going to do an invert, where you skated up toward the top of the ramp, grabbed the edge, and flipped over your arm before landing and skating back down. It was hard to do as a first trick, because it required a lot of speed. But I was certain I could pull it off.

I hit the ramp running as hard as I could and leaped onto my board. I was hurtling through the air as fast as I'd ever gone. It was like being on a motorcycle, the wind rushing all around me. I saw the lip of the ramp hurtling toward me at the speed of light. I bent low on the board, reached my arm out, and grabbed for the edge.

And I got it! Just like that I was in the air, rotating gracefully over my arm, my board stuck to my feet as though it was glued there. Far in the background I could hear the crowd cheering, but the blood pounding in my ears was even louder.

I landed the invert perfectly, rocketing back down the ramp. I ollied on the way down, leaping into the air and taking the board wi th me, then landing perfectly and continuing to skate as though I hadn't just flown through the air. I was on fire, hitting every trick perfectly. By the time I finished my fifth pass, I felt almost sorry for Lenni. It would be hard to follow me. But in a competition, there were always winners and losers.

I got off the ramp and stood by the side, near a few of the officials and other skaters who had finished their turns. David Sanders was there, walking lazily through the crowds and scoffing whenever someone missed a trick or slipped.

Lenni got up on the ramp. He seemed to ignore the crowd entirely. He stood completely still for a long moment, like a statue of a skater. Then he burst into motion.

He moved so fast I could barely see him. One second he was standing at the bottom of the ramp, the next he was riding his board up to the top. Then he seemed to slow down gracefully, doing an ollie in slow motion—a nearly impossible trick. It was a copycat of my first move, but I had to admit, he did it well.

And that was just the beginning. Lenni did kickflips and spins, tricks I'd never seen anyone do before. He even did a McTwist, flying up above the edge of the ramp and spinning over and over before coming back down and hurtling toward the center of the ramp, like a front flip while on a skateboard. For his final move, he leaped into the air on his way down the ramp, grabbed his board, and landed upside down in a one-handed hand-stand.

I whistled softly to myself.

"Wow," I said. "He totally blew me away."

"Yeah," said David. He'd come up from behind me, and I hadn't noticed him standing next to me. He had a nasty smirk on his face. "*She* did."

Beaten by a girl in the first round?

Burn!

FRANK

7

A Wolff in Sheep's Clothing

From the stands, I watched Joe get blown out of the water by his competition. By the end of the day, her name was on everyone's lips. Lenni Wolff. None of the other skaters had even heard of her, although that seemed impossible. Some people said she was as good as Cody himself. Others said she was better. One by one, she knocked down each of the skaters who came against her in the first round of trials. At first, people were paying attention to all the skating matches, but soon everyone was gathered around, waiting for her. Even Cody and London came down off the stage to get a better look. She had the highest standing by far when the competition ended for the day. There were a few other skaters who were in her league, but she was the odds-on favorite to win.

I went back and forth between watching her and watching the crowd, looking for any sign of Sk8rH8r, or the punks who had disrupted the park yesterday. But there was nothing, just an endless parade of people in Cody Zane shirts and hats. The competition seemed to go as smoothly as Tyrone could have wanted, and everyone seemed to be having a great time. Everyone except for Joe.

He was mopey all day after his loss. When I found him by the purple ramp right after he had skated and lost, he seemed in shock. He was standing there with his helmet in hand, mouth hanging open.

"You did well," I said, trying to cheer him up. It didn't work.

"Whatever," he said. "Besides, we're not really here for the competition. This was just so I could get close to Cody, remember?"

That wasn't what he'd said earlier, but I let it go. He and Lenni shook hands, and we walked off into the crowd. At first we split up, trying to cover more ground that way. Plus, I think Joe wanted some time to himself. But after an hour or two, he came and found me. He seemed to be in a much better mood. It's hard to stay sad for long when your day job is being an undercover detective and superspy. As the day went on, it became more and more obvious that nothing was going to happen, and we could take our time and watch the competition. Sk8rH8r and 4Real, whoever they were, seemed to be taking the day off.

Maybe, I thought, *the explosion of Mount McKenzie was a bomb planted long ago.* It could be that the case was over and we just didn't know it yet. But that didn't account for the razor-sharp metal strips on the ramp. Or the skateboarding protesters. Still, I could hope.

At the end of the day, Cody invited Lenni up on stage with him to congratulate her for winning the first round of the competition. Instead of using the stairs, she grabbed the front of the stage and hurtled up onto it, still wearing her skating pads and clutching her board. When she took off her helmet, she revealed short, spiky hair dyed a brilliant blue. Something about her looked familiar, but I couldn't think of what it was. Cody stepped up to the microphone.

"How about a big hand for today's top skater, Lenni Wolff!"

The crowd cheered, and Lenni waved once. She seemed tense—probably nervous over all the attention. This must have been her first time in a competition like this, which would explain why none of the other skaters had ever heard of her. Judging from her performance today, we'd be hearing a lot about her in the future.

"Lenni, eh? Funny name for a girl!"

Cody smiled his big celebrity grin at Lenni, but she just rolled her eyes at him. I imagined she heard jokes about her name a lot. He waited for a moment, expecting her to laugh or say something, but she just stood there silently.

"Well, yeah. Uh, as I was saying. A big hand for Lenni! She did some amazing stuff out there today. Truly impressive skating. The kind of thing I need to see for my new video game, Cody Zane: Skate or Die."

The crowd cheered at the mention of the game.

"In fact, the only way she could have skated better today would have been with a Hubris brand board. They're my brand of choice—in fact, I love them so much I'm the official spokes-skater for Hubris. Remember, with Hubris, you'll never fall!"

Jeez, I thought. *If he spent as much time skating as he does trying to sell stuff, he really would be an amazing skater.* So far I hadn't seen him skate even once!

Lenni seemed pretty bored by all his talk as well.

She kept looking up and around the stage. She was clearly uncomfortable up there. I almost felt bad for her. Being a great skater didn't automatically make you great at being the center of attention. Although it certainly seemed to help Cody. . . .

Finally Lenni had enough of Cody's speech. Right as Cody started talking about the benefits of drinking PowerUp, she walked over and took the mic from him. Cody looked shocked as she shooed him out of the way and took the podium for herself. For a moment the crowd went silent. Her nervousness suddenly took on a sinister feeling, as though she were waiting for something.

"Joe, look!" I pointed up above Lenni's head.

Two figures had appeared on the scaffolding above the stage, one on either side. Something was definitely wrong. Right as Lenni began to speak, they dropped something down.

A banner spread out below them, covering the entire back of the stage. In giant letters it read GAL-AXY X: ADVENTURE, OR ADVERTISING VENTURE?

"Cody here might tell you all about the companies that sponsor him," Lenni began to yell. "But what he isn't telling you is that Tyrone McKenzie stole this land! Myself and a bunch of other local skaters built a skate park here all by ourselves, and Tyrone McKenzie knocked it down and built a place where we have to pay to skate!"

I could see security guards looking around in confusion. In a few seconds Tyrone would have them charging the stage. But Lenni made the most of her moment.

"Cody Zane is a sellout for supporting Galaxy X! Has anyone here even seen him skate? All he cares about is the money—just like Tyrone McKenzie!"

They were coming for her now, a pack of guards on either side of the stage running her way. Joe and I were caught in the crowd and couldn't get near her. Lenni Wolff was about to go from top skater to top prisoner.

Or at least, it seemed that way. Right before the first of the guards reached her, Lenni threw the microphone down and shoved her helmet on. She took a running leap off the stage, throwing her board down in front of her. The crowd scattered to get out of her way.

The two figures on top of the scaffolding did the same thing, one jumping into the crowd on the right and one on the left. Suddenly I realized they were all dressed identically, in matching black outfits and the same helmet and knee pads. The crowd was moving to avoid being run over by Lenni and her friends or trampled by the guards, so Joe and I had a clear sight on the three of them.

"Come on!" I yelled to Joe. "We have to stop her—I mean, them—before they get away."

We ran toward Lenni and the other skaters. But we weren't the only ones. Out of the crowd came a dozen other skaters, all dressed in black with matching blue helmets. Within seconds it was impossible to tell which one of them was Lenni Wolff.

One came close to me and I tackled him. But once I got him to the ground, he pulled off his helmet and it was just some random boy. He stuck his tongue out at me and hopped back on his board, flying off in the direction the other skaters had gone. Joe had no luck either. He'd managed to get someone else off their skateboard, but though it was a girl, it certainly wasn't Lenni.

The security guards weren't even that successful. Once again, the skaters were flying rings around them, making the guards look like lumbering gorillas. Above it all I could hear Tyrone screaming, yelling abuse at the guards and Joe and me, offering a reward to anyone who could capture Lenni. But the crowd wasn't listening to him. They were too busy watching us make fools of ourselves.

Within a minute, all the skaters were gone. Up on the stage, Cody was still standing by the podium, shocked. The banner flapped in the wind above him. I could hear London's high, obnoxious laugh in the background. It looked like we had a new suspect number one.

Suspect Profile

<u>Name:</u> Lenni Wolff

<u>Hometown:</u> Right here on Coral Island, North Carolina—or what's left of it, after Tyrone demolished most of it to build Galaxy X.

<u>Occupation:</u> Professional troublemaker and amateur skater.

<u>Physical description:</u> 5'5"; 115 lbs; age 15; short, bright blue hair. Dresses like a skater: baggy jeans, big black boots, pins and patches on everything.

<u>Suspicious behavior:</u> She'd already disrupted Galaxy X and the Skate or Die Competition twice, and she clearly had an ax to grind with Cody Zane and Tyrone McKenzie. Maybe this skater was also a sk8rH8r?

<u>Suspected of</u>: Murdering Bret Johnston, and trying to sabotage the Cody Zane Skate or Die Competition.

<u>Possible motives</u>: Tyrone Smith leveled the skate park she had created in order to build Galaxy X. Plus, she seemed pretty angry at all the "poseurs" and "fakes" who were coming to skate at the competition.

The Ride of Their Lives

"Let's go after her! I mean, uh, them!" I yelled. In the distance, I could see the last of the blue-helmeted skaters zooming away through the park. But which one was Lenni? I couldn't tell them apart at all. It was a clever trick, that was for sure.

"Forget it, Joe," said Frank. "There's no way we can catch up with them. Besides, it looks like Cody is heading off into the park—we should follow him."

I turned around and saw that Frank was right—Cody, London, and David seemed to be heading out of the competition area and into the heart of Galaxy X. Cody's bodyguards had been distracted by chasing Lenni, and it looked like Cody was taking advantage of their absence to get some time on his own. We couldn't let him wander off in the park with Lenni and her gang of skaters on the loose. I also saw Tyrone heading our way, looking madder than ever. Luckily, he was having a hard time getting through the crowd. With Frank right behind me, I hustled over to reach Cody and get out of Tyrone's way. I don't think he was too pleased with how the competition had gone. We leaped up onto the stage and followed Cody out the back exit before Tyrone could reach us.

"Hey, guys!" As usual, Cody seemed to be in a good—if somewhat spacey—mood. If he was upset by what had happened at the competition, he didn't show it.

"That was far out!" London laughed. "All that 'blah blah blah' speech making . . . and that crazy chase was like . . . wow!"

David grunted sourly.

It was business as usual with the Zaniacs.

"Want to come ride some roller coasters with us?" Cody asked. "We're going to see if we can hit all the major ones in a single afternoon. First person to puke owes everyone ice cream!"

"Sounds great," I agreed. Frank looked a little

green at the mention of the rides, but he agreed to come too. Only David hung back.

"I was thinking maybe we could, I don't know—skate or something?" David sounded irritated. "Remember, that thing we used to do together?"

Cody just laughed. "That's cool, dude. Have fun practicing."

He held up his hand for a high five, but David was already stalking off toward the VIP area. I don't think I'd seen him smile once yet. Cody shrugged and tried to laugh it off, but I could tell he was kind of upset. All the magazines and websites said David and Cody had been best friends who grew up skating together, but it certainly seemed like their relationship had gone sour.

Cody had a map of the park and a list of rides he wanted to go on. He wasn't kidding—he really loved roller coasters. The scarier the better. He skipped all the easy ones. If it didn't flip upside down or drop you a hundred feet, he wasn't really interested. London, too—the crazier the ride, the more into it she was.

"We'll do this one as a warm-up," Cody said, pointing to a ride called the Whirligig.

"Lead the way," said Frank. He was definitely looking a little woozy. He could fly a plane or go on a motorcycle chase, no problem, but he wasn't a big fan of roller coasters.

The Whirligig turned out to be a giant tower that rose forty feet up in the air. Dozens of cables hung down from it like tentacles off of a giant squid. Each person was suited up in a special vest, and a cable was connected to their back. When the ride started, the tower began to twist in place, spinning faster and faster until Cody, Joe, London, and I were all dragged off our feet. Soon we were flying through midair like Superman.

"YEAAAHHH!"

I could hear Cody whooping and hollering. The faster we went, the louder he yelled. London's mockingbird laugh could be heard even over his yelling. I was dizzy by the time the ride finally let us down, and Frank could barely stand up. But Cody and London got off and immediately started running to the next ride.

"Let's do that one!" London pointed to a ride where the cars were all shaped like giant snakes. The whole roller coaster looked vaguely snakelike, all shiny black and green with an S-shaped track. Appropriately, it was called the Cobra.

It whipped around the track so fast I thought it was going to break my neck. I'd flown in jets that I would swear hadn't gone that fast. As you rode, the car made a terrible hissing noise, exactly like a giant snake. It was awesome!

We went on four or five more rides in rapid succession. The best part about being with Cody was that everyone got right out of his way—we never waited on a single line. Sometimes we got mobbed by autograph seekers, but mostly people were excited just to point at Cody and whisper to their friends. Every boy in the park wanted a picture with London. And some girl even asked Cody to marry her!

"I'm hungry," London announced as we got off a ride that was like a cross between a Ferris wheel and a roller coaster—each car rotated around in a circle while zooming down a giant track. Frank seemed nauseated at even the mention of food.

"I want to keep riding. Joe, bud, would you take London to get something to eat? I wouldn't want her to get lonely." Cody threw his arm around London's shoulders, and she giggled.

"Sure." I was having a blast riding the coasters with Cody, and I didn't really want to stop. But he asked me specifically, so I didn't feel like I could say no. Besides, we were buds now, and this was the sort of thing buds did for each other.

"Uh . . . I could get food with London." Frank tried to break in, but everyone ignored him.

Soon London and I were on our way to the All-You-Can-Eat Fried Everything stand, while Frank and Cody wandered over to the entrance of the Leap.

The Leap was Galaxy X's most infamous roller coaster. It was one of a kind. From a distance, it looked like two roller coasters standing next to each other. The cars zoomed around the first one, building up speed until they were sent rocketing off in midair, before landing safely on the second coaster.

At least, that was how it was supposed to be. It looked like the Leap wasn't open yet. But while London debated between getting a fried Twinkie on a stick or a breaded and deep-fried chicken wing, I watched as a maintenance man ran down to let Cody and Frank into the ride. I guess being Cody Zane had its perks.

London and I sat by one of the tall tables and watched as the Leap cranked itself to life to send its first riders over its "Chasm of Doom." I had to admit, I was kind of jealous of Frank at that moment.

"That's funny," London said to herself as she chowed down on her Twinkie stick.

"What?"

"The angle of the roller coaster. If I were

approaching that jump on my board, I would say there was no way I could make it."

I looked at the place where the two halves of the Leap faced each other. London was right. The launching half was much lower than the landing half. If the coaster actually went around the track and over the jump, it would be cut in two by the steel rails on the other side—along with anyone in the car!

I was running toward the ride before I even had time to think about what I was going to do. I heard London yelling after me, but I didn't have time to explain. If I didn't hurry, Frank and Cody were going to have the ride of their lives—the *last* ride of their lives, that is.

Before I could get to the Leap, the cars began moving. Cody and Joe were in the second car sent around the coaster. There was an empty car half-way around the track already. I tried yelling up to the operator, but the little booth was perched too far up for them to hear me. Frank and Cody began to gain speed, flying through the first loop of the track. I could hear Cody screaming with joy. I had maybe fifteen seconds to save them. Maybe.

My eyes darted around the roller coaster, look-ing for some way to stop it. By the time I climbed up to the operator's booth, it would be too late. How could I stop a thousand pounds of speeding metal?

Suddenly I spotted a series of thick cables leading from the machinery of the coaster to a giant power generator nearby. If I could cut off the electricity, it might stop the car before it was too late.

I was closing in on the generator when the first empty car shot out between the two halves of the Leap. For a second it looked as though it was going to make it—then it dipped too low and rammed straight into the other side of the ride. With a horrible screeching noise, the track went through the car like a knife through butter. A rain of sparks and shrapnel came hailing down on me. Something sharp sliced my arm, but I kept running. All around me, people were pointing and screaming.

When the generator was just a few feet in front of me, I dove through the air. I slammed shoulder first into the wires, ripping them out of the machine. All around me, I heard the sounds of carnival music slowing down eerily and stopping. Lights flickered and went out.

I landed heavily on the ground, knocking the wind out of me. By the time I stood up, Frank and Cody's car had already begun to slow down. But they were awfully close to the edge already. It didn't look like they were going to stop in time. I had failed—and Cody and Frank were about to pay the price.

FRANK
9

Leap of Faith

It was funny that I was going to die on a roller coaster, since I've always hated them so much. Motorcycles? Great. Hang gliders? Love them. Riding unbroken horses without a saddle? Lead me to it. But something about roller coasters always icked me out. I tried to hide my happiness when I saw that the Leap was closed, but then that guy had to come and let us in.

"Hey," he had yelled. "You're Cody Zane! For you, all the rides are open." Then he and Cody high-fived. Cody pulled a marker from his pocket and wrote "Zaniac" on the back of the man's T-shirt, and next thing I knew we were being buckled into the car. The mechanic assured us the ride was set to go—he had finished testing it that morning. He had just gotten back from lunch and was about to send one final test car around the ride, but we could go along for the ride in a second car.

Cody was psyched. "I've been reading about the Leap for a year—there's nothing else like it out there. And we're going to be the first to ride it!"

Just the thought of it made my stomach churn. I'd have given anything to be down there eating fries with Joe and London. Once the ride started up, though, it wasn't that bad. Cody was screaming and laughing, and after I managed to stop holding the safety bar so hard my hands hurt, I started to get into it, too.

Maybe roller coasters aren't so bad, I thought.

That's when, out of the corner of my eye, I noticed Joe running. I couldn't figure out what he was doing, but I knew right away that something was wrong. I tried to stand up as much as I could, to get a better view of the park and the ride ahead of us, but the seat belt had me stuck to the seat. But as soon as I looked, I saw that the problem was the angle of the tracks. It was simple geometry. Simple but deadly.

"Whoa. Calm down, man—it's all good." Cody patted me on the shoulder and laughed. He hadn't noticed Joe and had no idea that anything was wrong. Then the first car went over the break in the tracks and slammed into the other side. It exploded in sparks and pieces of metal. Cody screamed again, but this time he sounded more shocked and confused than excited and amused.

Now I understood why Joe was running. I spotted the power generator right ahead of him. But even if he made it there before we went over the ledge, the momentum the car had gathered already would be enough to send us crashing to our deaths. Then I saw it—our one chance of making it off this roller coaster alive. I pulled out my pocket knife and sliced through the restraints that held Cody and me in our seats.

"Careful, dude." Cody seemed more worried by my knife than by our impending crash. He still didn't get it, even though we'd watched the other car explode.

"On the count of three," I told him, "we're going to jump for that scaffolding over there."

Right before the break in the tracks, there was scaffolding that extended up above the roller coaster to give it extra support. It would be a dangerous jump, but staying in the car meant certain death.

"Wicked, man," said Cody. "Let's do it!"

I tried not to roll my eyes at the excitement in his voice. Didn't he take anything seriously?

"Ready? One . . . two . . . three!"

Cody and I leaped out of our seats.

I just barely managed to grasp the metal scaffolding up above. There was a tremendous crashing sound as our car slammed into the other end of the Leap, then an even louder smash as it hit the ground and shattered into a million pieces. Bits of metal were flying through the air. Then my right hand slipped, and I thought I would go plunging down and land on the crushed wreckage of the roller coaster car below. I swung back and forth in midair, my right arm windmilling as I tried to grab hold of the bar. Then Cody reached out and pulled me up.

"Careful," he said, and grinned at me.

There was nothing to be done but hang there until help arrived to pull us down. I looked around at the roller coaster. Without getting closer, I couldn't see if there was any evidence of who had sabotaged the ride, but I could see how they had done it. Someone had jacked up the other side of the ride using a series of small cranks and pulleys, turning the Leap into the Guillotine. Whoever had pulled this off certainly knew a lot about machines. They must have done it while the mechanic was on his lunch break, which meant they worked fast.

From a distance I could hear the howling of sirens, and soon I saw a fleet of fire trucks on their way. They had TYRONE written on the side of them in huge red, white, and blue letters.

Wow, I thought. *Tyrone really* does *own the whole island.*

From this high up I could see that ours was not the only ride having problems. Whether it was because of the electrical cords Joe had pulled or sabotage, rides all over the park were frozen, or moving backward, or had their lights blinking on and off.

I felt a rush of air at my side and turned to find Cody falling off the scaffolding!

Or at least, that's what it looked like. Then he shot one hand out and caught himself again. Then he started doing flips, pulling himself up to the bar and swinging his entire body around. It was like he was a gymnast. And he was enjoying himself. He was actually *laughing*! A crowd had gathered below us, and I could see people pulling out their cell phones and taking videos of Cody.

"You know," Cody said, in between tricks, "I bet Tyrone needs to do some commercials for this place. You know, some action shots, something for MTV. Up here would totally be a great place to shoot. Do some skate tricks off the roller coaster track? It would be hot! And I'd love to star in them. For the right price, of course. My agent would have to negotiate that. But I could totally be the face of this place, easy."

I felt something buzzing in my pocket. In all the excitement of the past few hours, I'd totally forgotten about Tyrone's PDA. Carefully I put one hand in my pocket and pulled it out. It was a message from our old friend Sk8rH8r.

CLOSE THE PARK—OR I'LL CLOSE IT FOR U. 1 RIDE AT A TIME.

Stage Fright

"**M**an, could today get any worse?" I flopped down on my bed in the Galaxy X hotel room that Tyrone had set us up in. "Our main suspect managed to totally escape and make us look like idiots, you nearly got killed by a roller coaster. And the screaming. The way Tyrone carried on, you'd think we made the Leap malfunction ourselves."

Frank nodded. "Yeah. And don't forget the part where you totally got your butt handed to you on a platter during the Skate or Die Competition. By a girl."

I threw a pillow at him, and he ducked out of the way. We had a little time to relax before the big event tonight: the Galaxy X Blastoff, a giant concert being headlined by Mr. Nice Guyz. Cody was going to be the emcee, and our old friend Kijani and her band the Royal We were also performing. Tyrone had envisioned it as a huge party to celebrate the opening of the park, but the word going around Galaxy X was that most people were attending just to see what would go wrong. Already, rumors of a curse on the park were starting to spread, as one thing after another malfunctioned, got disrupted or just outright exploded. Frank and I decided to spend our free time trying to figure out who could be behind all of it. If we didn't get a lead soon, I was going to start believing in ghosts.

"Seriously, though," I said. "What is going on here? I thought we had everything in hand when we arrested Wallace. He admitted to making that fake bomb and to messing up our dune buggy. But we haven't been able to catch a break since."

I was getting frustrated.

"Well, whoever's behind this has to have pretty full access to the park," said Frank. "Otherwise how would they be able to plant a bomb on Mount McKenzie, or sabotage the rides before the park had even officially opened?"

"Right. That sounds like Bret Johnston to me.

But it also has to be someone who's pretty tricky. Some of those traps were clever and hard to pull off, like what happened with The Leap."

"And that points to Lenni. Bret doesn't seem like the brightest crayon in the box, if you know what I mean."

We were getting nowhere. Both of them seemed suspicious, but neither was the perfect suspect. We needed some hard evidence, or to catch one of them in the act of sabotaging the park or something.

"Well, if I had to bet on one, I'd go for Lenni," I said.

Frank started laughing at me. I realized how that sounded.

"And not just because she beat me! She's got a better motive, and we already know that there are people out there willing to destroy the park because of how and where Tyrone built it. Maybe she's in league with Wallace somehow."

"Well, whoever it was, it feels like things are getting more and more dangerous. That malfunction on the Leap today could have killed somebody! And Tyrone says it wasn't the only ride to break. Three other rides stopped working too. We'd better head over to the Blastoff and make sure nothing happens there."

"Yeah. If anything else goes wrong, we'll have at least one death on our hands."

Frank looked at me. "Huh?" he said. "Whose?"

"Tyrone's—if he gets any more upset, his head is definitely going to blow off."

Thankfully, most of the night attractions in the park weren't up and running yet, so we didn't have to worry about any other "accidents" while the Blastoff was going on. Our only job tonight was to watch out for Cody and make sure the party went off without a hitch. Tyrone had issued us both backstage passes. As usual, he'd pulled out all the stops. Instead of the usual plastic badges or wristbands, these passes were giant golden keys on long necklaces. They were so heavy, I suspected they might be *actual* gold. "Subtle" was a concept Tyrone didn't understand.

We flashed our keys to the security guards around the concert arena and were quickly ushered past the crowds milling outside, waiting for the event to begin. The backstage was packed wall-to-wall with celebrities, journalists, sound techs, and instruments.

"Frank! Joe!" A beautiful and slightly accented voice called out to us from behind a ring of reporters and cameras. A hand emerged from the circle, then an arm, and then suddenly Kijani, lead singer of the Royal We, came bursting out. She nearly tackled me with a hug. Within seconds, we were enveloped in press as well, with camera flashes going off everywhere.

"What are you two doing here?" Kijani asked. Her left hand was holding my hand and her right arm was around Frank's shoulders. Suddenly the smile left her face. Kijani had been a target in a case we had worked on before, at a big concert just like this.

"Uh, well, we—I mean, that is . . ."

Frank's kind of like Superman—and girls are his kryptonite. I leaped in to save him, before Kijani said anything about us and ATAC.

"Oh, you know—we love concerts. Like at Rockapazooma, remember?"

Rockapazooma was the big rock festival at which we had met Kijani. I hoped she got the hint—I didn't want her to say anything or ask any more questions in front of all the reporters.

"Oh! Yes, I remember." Kijani looked even more worried now. She must have assumed we were investigating another plot against her. I rushed to reassure her.

"Anyway, we're just here taking care of our friend Cody Zane."

Kijani's eyes went wide, but the scared expression left her face. "If there is anything I can do," she began, and trailed off. She knew the kind of criminals we took on. They were pretty dangerous folks, and not anyone people who weren't ATAC trained should try to take on.

"Thanks," Frank managed to squeak out.

Near the stage, someone yelled Kijani's name.

"I must go do my sound check. Keep safe, both of you." She squeezed my hand, then leaned in to give Frank a kiss on the cheek. Typical. Girls love the silent type.

Everything was in full swing, and it seemed like the concert was going to start any minute. I could hear the fans in the audience, chanting for Bret Johnston. Mr. Nice Guyz was headlining the show tonight. That would give us a chance to keep an eye on Bret as well as Cody. MNG's fans were pretty crazy—girls had been showing up with giant signs and life-size cutouts of Bret all day. There were rumors that they might try to rush the stage, which was exactly the sort of chaos that would give Sk8rH8r or 4Real the chance to cause some serious mischief.

Frank and I were walking backstage, trying to find Cody, when I noticed someone moving in the rafters above us. I squinted up. There were roadies and stage crew everywhere, but something about the way this person was moving made it seem like they were trying to stay hidden. A spotlight was turned on, and I caught just a hint of bright blue hair before the person scurried back into the shadow. It was Lenni!

I nudged Frank in the side and casually gestured upward with my eyebrows. He understood what I meant. Quickly we split up. I moved to the right. Once I judged that I was out of Lenni's line of sight, I started climbing. On the other side of the stage, Frank did the same. If we were quick enough, we could have her trapped before she had any idea we were even there.

Something must have tipped her off, though, because before I reached the top of the pillar she was already running across the rafters. She was incredibly fast and had amazing balance. But Frank and I were on two sides of her, and there was only so far she could go before the stage ended. As soon as she tried to start climbing down, we'd be on her.

In the noise and the excitement of the concert starting, no one even looked up as Frank, Lenni, and I ran and leaped all over the metal beams above the stage. Finally we cornered her on one long stretch of pipe. I was at one end, Frank was at the other, and we had Lenni in the middle.

"Give yourself up," Frank yelled.

Distantly in the background I heard Cody's name announced and the crowd go wild. The concert must have been starting. Frank and I edged closer in on the beam, penning Lenni in between us.

KKKRRRRRZZZZZZZT!!!

A tremendous electrical shrieking noise came through all the speakers for a second, with a human scream almost drowned out beneath it. The lights and the music cut out all at once, and the entire stage was plunged into darkness.

One thought raced through my mind:

Cody!

Short Circuit

In the dark, I felt something slam into me. It must have been Lenni rushing past. For a moment I lost my balance. I windmilled my arms, trying desperately to stay upright, but I felt myself start to fall. I couldn't even make out the stage below me in the darkness, but I knew it was a long way down.

Thankfully, a hand shot out and pulled me back up on to the beam. "Joe?" I said. I heard a girl's laughter and a patter of running footsteps, and then Lenni was gone. I started to chase her, but in the dark, I knew it would be too dangerous.

"Frank?" Joe called out from the other side of the beam. "You okay?"

"Yeah—but I think Lenni just got away. What's going on?"

I carefully inched my way across the beam to Joe's side. From here, we could see that the lights hadn't gone out only in the concert arena—the entire park appeared to be enveloped in darkness. All around the arena, people were screaming and running. Even in the dark, the stage looked to be utter chaos.

"Something's happened to Cody!" said Joe. "We have to get down there."

In the dark, scrabbling down the metal scaffolding was dangerous and slow going. More than once we had to backtrack and find a different way to descend. Joe was getting more and more impatient by the second. Finally, when we got about six feet above the stage, Joe leaped right off the scaffolding.

We raced to the front of the stage, where a circle of people had gathered in the midst of the larger craziness. I saw Erica, Tyrone, Nick, Kijani, and a bunch of other celebrities who had shown up for the grand opening—but there was no sign of Cody. They were all clustered around . . . *something*. I squinted, and saw a leg sticking out at a strange angle. Someone was lying on the ground in the middle of the circle, and it didn't look like they were moving.

Cody!

Joe and I ran toward them. We broke past the gathered people to find Cody kneeling over Bret Johnston.

"He—I mean, I tried to give him CPR, but . . . he's not breathing!"

I led Cody away by the arm while Joe took his place. ATAC trained us in first aid and emergency medicine. If there was anything that could be done, Joe would do it. But I was pretty sure from looking at Bret that it was already too late. Joe was pushing on his chest and breathing into his mouth. I tried to question Cody.

"What happened?"

"I don't know, man. One second they were calling my name and I was walking out on stage. Then, bam! Bret ran right into me and shoved me out of the way. I hit the floor, and the next thing I knew, Bret screamed and the lights went out and—I tried to help him, man, I really did."

Erica came over to where we were. She was crying into her hands.

"He—he—he said that it wasn't fair and that it was his concert and *he* should be the first one on the stage. I said he should go for it, because I just wanted him to leave me alone, but he did it!

He ran out and grabbed the microphone, and as soon as he touched it the speakers exploded and he screamed."

Erica was crying harder now, and I reached out to pat her on the arm. She flung herself at me, crying on my shoulder. I didn't know what to do, so I stroked her hair to calm her down. She cried for a minute more, and then started to pull herself together.

"Joe, we need to get everyone away from the sound system and get the power turned off," I yelled out, but Joe couldn't hear me. He had his cell phone out, and it looked like he was requesting an ambulance from 911.

"I can do that," said Erica. Her face was still wet and her eyes red, but she had managed to stop crying.

"Are you sure?"

"Yeah—I was here when they put the system in place. I know how it's rigged up. It'll just take me a minute."

She ran off toward the back of the stage, and I joined Joe at Bret's side. Bret's skin was gray, and he still wasn't breathing. This close to him, I could smell singed hair and see the burn marks on his hands. The crowd of people was inching in closer, trying to see if Joe had managed to revive Bret.

"Everyone back up!" I shouted. We needed some room. "And no one touch any of the wires!"

Tyrone sent out some of his guards to quiet the crowd and start escorting people out of the stadium. A ragged chant of "Cody, Cody, Cody" went up for a while, but soon even the die-hard fans gave up and left.

Soon Erica came running back.

"The power's shut off."

"Thanks." I walked over to where the microphone had rolled from Bret's limp, dead hand. I put the back of my hand against it, carefully, just to make sure there was no electricity running through it.

"Careful!" Cody said. He had followed behind me and seemed horrified that I had touched the microphone.

"It's okay. When you get an electric shock, it causes your muscles to contract. If I touched it the normal way, with the tips of my fingers or the palm of my hand, the contraction would make me grab the microphone and be unable to let go. Then the electricity would go right through me. When I touch it with the back of my hand, if there is still electricity running through it, the current would cause my hand to contract, pushing it *away* from the microphone. That's why you always touch electrical things with the back of your hand."

If Cody was to stay alive, we might have to teach him a few things. Not that it mattered in this case. Erica had done the job perfectly, and the microphone had no electricity going through it. I lifted it up and examined the place where the electrical cord met the base. There was no doubt about it. Someone had stripped the wires, leaving the copper underneath bare and dangerous to the touch. But there was something else. I had to squint to read it, but in small letters, someone had scratched the word "sellout" into the side of the microphone.

Cody saw what I was looking at.

"Dude . . . someone did this on purpose!"

His face fell, and his skin took on a greenish color. He looked like he might throw up.

"Frank—this is serious. Those messages weren't kidding. I think someone might be trying to kill me!"

12

Fired

Once the ambulance had come and taken Bret Johnston's body away, we grabbed Cody and pulled him to the back of the stage to ask him about the mysterious "messages" he had mentioned to Frank.

"You've been getting what?" I asked, shocked at what Cody had told us.

"Death threats," he said. "For . . . I dunno. A month, maybe two." Cody looked embarrassed when he said it. And well he should be. He knew about the accidents that had been happening, the investigation that was underway. It was crazy that he had kept this from us.

"What did the threats say?" asked Frank.

"Oh, man . . . all sorts of stuff. How I was a sellout, and I'd forgotten everything that used to matter to me, and I was so fake all the time. Really negative stuff, you know? Not nice at all."

"Mr. Zane, sir?"

Two of Cody's bodyguards came up while we were talking. They were like mountains in suits. Their shoulders were so big their heads looked like tiny little toys perched on top.

"Eddie, Gilbert—how's it going, guys?"

Cody offered his hand for a high-five, and after an awkward pause, one of the two men very carefully touched his palm lightly. He had hands so large they made Cody look like a child.

"We'll have to ask you to come with us back to your hotel, sir. This area is not secure."

They could say that again! Tyrone was trying to get everyone out of the arena, but the lights hadn't come back on yet, and Lenni was still out there somewhere. We needed to get Cody to safety, fast.

"I'll go with you," I volunteered. "Frank, you stay here and—"

"Mr. Zane will be coming with us by himself."

I looked at Cody. This was ridiculous! I was his friend. Moreover, ATAC had assigned me to this case. Surely I was better protection than some muscle-bound thug!

"Sorry, Joe, they work for my manager. Got to listen to what they say." Cody shrugged his shoulders regretfully, but he looked glad to be getting out of there. The two bodyguards walked on either side of him and whisked him off the stage and out of the arena double time.

"Well, that all sounded pretty familiar," Frank said.

"Yeah. Those death threats have Lenni written all over them. I can't believe she got away from us tonight!"

"And how did she manage to get down on the stage to strip those wires without anyone noticing? Tyrone's guards aren't the best, but they're not blind."

I shook my head. She was clever, that was for sure. I wasn't looking forward to telling Tyrone about all this.

"What? This girl was at the scene of the crime and you didn't catch her?" Tyrone seemed upset, to put it mildly. Judging from the look of his office, we'd arrived shortly after he'd finished throwing things. His books were in heaps all over the floor, his cell phone was embedded in one wall, and his computer had been smashed into a million pieces. At first I thought someone had ransacked his office, but then I realized he had done it himself.

He looked like he wanted to throw me right now. I'd just finished telling him about chasing Lenni through the rafters right before Bret Johnston was electrocuted. He grew really quiet for a second—scary quiet. Then he blew up again.

"Those stupid protesters! Those—those—kids with their dinky little skateboard ramps! I built twenty ramps here, all of them bigger—all of them better—than the ones they had made. So what if they have to pay to get in! That's how the world works. They should stop spending all their time skating and get jobs—then they could use the park just fine! They are ruining my profit margins!"

I couldn't believe it. Tyrone still seemed more concerned about his money than about the lives of the people visiting Galaxy X—including his own children. I still hadn't forgotten that rock the protesters had thrown at Erica's head when we first got here. She was lucky it hadn't been something more serious. And Bret Johnston was dead. Didn't Tyrone realize that this wasn't a game anymore?

"I think this makes things pretty obvious," Frank said. "You need to call off the competition and shut down the park until we can catch Lenni."

"What?" Tyrone said. Then he started laughing. It was a mean laugh. "Shut the park down? Do you have any idea how much money I would lose?"

"Well, you've at least got to put off the competition. Bret's dead—Cody could be next."

"You're out of your mind, kid. That's what I have the two of you here for. To keep people like her from messing up my park! But you know what? You two can't even handle that."

Tyrone paused for a moment. Then a look came over his face, like a lightbulb going off. He snapped his fingers.

"Forget it. Don't bother. You're out of a job. Since you two can't hack it, I'm bringing in private security. This is a job for men. I don't know what I was thinking, hiring two *boys* to try to guard my investment."

"But—you can't do that." I couldn't believe Tyrone was pulling us off the case. We'd already captured one of the people responsible for sabotaging the park, and we almost had the other. Taking us off the case now was just . . . stupid.

Tyrone barely heard me. He was busy prying his cell phone out of the wall. He flipped it open to check if it still worked, then dialed a number.

"Yeah," he said into the phone. "Ox. We need to talk about additional security guards. I'm going to need, like, a hundred more—starting tomorrow."

He paused for a second, seeming to remember Frank and I were there.

"You two can stay until tomorrow—but after that, I want you gone."

We stared at him, too shocked to say anything.

"Get out!" he screamed, and we did.

We walked back to our rooms in stunned silence. The last two hours were like a bad dream. Bret Johnston was dead. The concert was canceled. Lenni had somehow managed to get away from us in the dark. And now Tyrone was hiring a bunch of security guards to replace us!

"I think we just got fired," Frank said when we finally arrived.

"Yeah. I can't believe it."

"Those security guards aren't going to be able to catch Lenni. She can ride rings around them."

I knew from going up against her in the competition that Lenni was an amazing athlete. She'd even managed to get away from us repeatedly, which is pretty impressive, considering how awesome I was. Frank too.

"That's why we've got to catch her. We've only got twenty-four hours to do it, so we'd better get started."

I called ATAC and told them we needed an immediate search run on "Lenni Wolff." I gave them all the information we had, which wasn't much. They'd let us know if she had a police record, or any other criminal history. We just had to hope that was her real name.

"Take a look at this," said Frank. He'd booted up the laptop ATAC had given us and done some searching on the Internet. One of the most frequent posters on StopGX.com went by the name "Sk8Wolff." It wasn't hard to figure out who that was.

She also had her own blog, which was mostly pictures of her skating with the other skaters we'd seen at the first protest. There were some rants up there about Galaxy X and Tyrone as well. More of what we'd heard already, about how the skaters supporting Galaxy X were sellouts and phonies.

"There's a lot more, too. It looks like Lenni is as active on the Internet as she is at Galaxy X."

Frank pulled up a ton of other blogs, websites, and posts from Sk8Wolff. Seems like Lenni was pretty politically active. She had written stuff against animal cruelty and sweatshop labor, and a lot of stuff about how biking (and skateboarding) were better for the environment than cars. When she wasn't screaming in all caps, she actually sounded pretty smart.

My phone rang, and Frank and I both jumped,

expecting more bad news from Tyrone. Instead it was ATAC on the line. Lenni had an arrest record—but all for peaceful protest activities. She was passionate about her beliefs, but she'd never been violent. At least, up until now.

In fact, from everything we read, she seemed like a pretty cool person . . . except that all the evidence suggested she had just killed Bret Johnston.

Gorillas in Their Midst

The morning after the Blastoff turned into the Blackout, the park was a different place. There had been one too many accidents for most people. On opening day, people had been lined up to get into the park. Now, they were lining up to get out. Whole areas of the park were nearly empty. Rides went around with only one or two people on them. Everyone seemed on edge.

The new park guests who had arrived that morning were very different from the thrill seekers and athletes who had come for the opening. These were people attracted by the "cursed" reputation that was already growing around Galaxy X. Some of them seemed to be looking for trouble.

And then there were Tyrone's new guards. I didn't think he'd be able to rustle up one hundred of them overnight, but I guess with enough money, anything was possible. Each one was larger, scarier, and dumber than the last. Most of them were so huge that they didn't fit into the spare uniforms. They looked like adults wearing clothes from the toddler section: tiny shirts and miniature pants that ended above their ankles.

"Look," Joe said when we first saw them. "Tyrone's cloned cavemen! Or are those just gorillas in uniforms?"

We were walking toward the Skate or Die Competition when we first ran into them. Three of the guards had surrounded a group of guys who had been yelling and throwing popcorn at one another.

"Chill, man," one of the guys said. He was clearly one of the people who'd arrived looking for the park to be a disaster and was spoiling for a fight. He flicked some popcorn in the face of the guard who had been talking to him. Bad move to pull on a guy who's six inches taller than you.

The guard shoved the guy as hard as he could, sending him flying backward into his friends. The other two guards laughed as he sprawled on the ground. As he got up, his friends spread out, their hands curled into fists. One picked up a tree branch that was lying in the grass nearby. This wasn't looking good.

"That's funny," I said. "I thought the security guards were supposed to stop fights, not pick them."

"Looks like we'd better give them a hand. I've got an idea."

Joe ran over to them right before they started trading punches.

"Hey!" he yelled. "I hear that the Fun House just caught fire! It's insane. They want all security over there ASAP."

The guards looked like they'd rather fight than do their jobs. But they weren't the ones Joe was really trying to convince.

"A fire?" one of the visitors said. "That's what I'm here for. Let's go check it out!"

Like that, the guys scattered, all wanting to see the disaster in action. Galaxy X seemed to have a way of bringing out the worst in people. The guards still seemed ready to start a fight, so Joe and I got out of the way as fast as we could. Soon we were over at the skate park, just in time for the start of the competition.

There was still a crowd here. Even last night's disaster couldn't keep the top competitors from trying for a place in the new Skate or Die video game. But someone *was* missing. Up on the stage, I saw Cody and David, but there was no sign of London.

"Joe—London's gone!" I wondered if something had happened to her in the night.

"Yeah, didn't you guys hear?" The girl in front of us in the crowd turned around. "She had to go to Milan for, like, a modeling emergency. She flew out late last night. She is so committed. She's my role model."

I tried not to roll my eyes. "Modeling emergency." Yeah, right. But I couldn't really blame her—Galaxy X was turning out to be a pretty dangerous place for celebrities. At least it was one less person we had to keep an eye on today.

We headed toward the judges' table, hoping to talk to Cody before the competition began. We made it as far as the gate.

"Sorry, Mr. McKenzie's orders," said a mountain in a Galaxy X uniform. "You two are no longer allowed backstage."

"What? But we're the ones who've been keeping Cody safe this entire time." I couldn't believe they were going to stop us from going back there.

"Yeah, and you've been doing a great job at that." The mountain laughed with a sound like an avalanche starting deep in his chest. Joe decided to try a different approach.

"Look, Cody is a personal friend of mine, and—"

The guard cut him off. "I don't care if you're his mother. You're not getting backstage."

"Come on, Joe. The event's about to start anyway. Let's find someplace where we can at least see Cody."

I guess Tyrone was serious about wanting us gone. We got back to the crowd just in time to see Cody step up to the platform. There was no big speech this time. Cody looked scared.

"Good luck, guys!" he said. He waved to the crowd once, and a small cheer went up. Then he scurried back to the chair he had been sitting in, and his bodyguards surrounded him again.

With that, the competition was officially on. There were only twenty-five contenders in this round, and so each one went separately. This was the trick portion of the competition. Each competitor had five minutes to show off the most impressive, interesting, and exciting moves in their arsenal. It was also their chance to show off their personal style. Cody was looking for someone who was not only a great skater, but also had a great personality—someone who would make a fun character to play in the game.

Some of the competitors had gone to great lengths to stand out. One guy was skating in a giant chicken costume, which probably seemed like a brilliant idea until the mask covered his eyes mid-skate and he went down hard. A girl named Rose showered the crowd with rose petals while in the middle of a backflip on her board, which scored her big points with both the audience and the judges. Others skated while playing ukuleles, or with crazy face paint on, or on boards that were longer and thinner than usual.

At the halfway point of the competition, a break was announced to allow the crowd to get some food and hang out with the contestants.

"I'm going to get some curly fries," I told Joe. "You want anything?"

"No. I think I'm going to go introduce myself to Rose."

Joe had that look in his eye—the one that says he's feeling particularly slick. Usually it lasted all of ten minutes before the girls shot him down, but Joe was nothing if not optimistic. I headed off to find some lunch while he worked his away over to the contestant area.

The food stands surrounded the skating area, selling everything from milkshakes to pizza to hot dogs. I followed the smell of deep frying until I found the Fry Boy. I was just about to get in line when someone slammed into me from behind, hard. I fell down on my hands and knees.

"Sorry, sorry—oh, man, I'm so sorry." I heard a woman's voice and felt the hands of the assembled crowd helping me to my feet. By the time I got up, whoever it was who had run in to me was gone. And so was my cell phone.

It was a classic move—knocking someone over and then robbing them while you pretend to help them up. I couldn't believe it had happened to me. I searched my bag over and over again, but there was no question. I had been pickpocketed! Thankfully, I still had my wallet, but our cell phones were specially made for us by ATAC and could do a ton of things that a normal phone couldn't. I had no doubt that they cost a fortune to replace. Joe and I already had a reputation in ATAC for having our gear lost, stolen, or destroyed during our investigations. Mostly it was because we took on the toughest cases . . . but it didn't stop other agents from giving us a hard time about it.

Since I'd already come this far and there was pretty much nothing I could do about my phone, I got fries anyway. Then I headed back to find Joe.

"Bummer," he said, when I told him about the robbery. "You'll be able to get a new one soon, though, since it looks like we're headed home today anyway."

Joe pulled a fry from my basket and started chowing down. Then he paused.

"Mmmph!" he said.

"What?"

"MMMPH!"

This time he pointed behind me. I turned and saw a commotion over by the competition ramp. Someone was doing some pretty good skating, which was strange, since the competition hadn't restarted yet and no one had been announced. People had gathered around and were applauding as the skater did flips and stalls and even leaped off the board and moonwalked at one point, only to hop back on as the board came hurtling by.

The skater flew up toward the top of the ramp and stopped in a handstand position, his board on his feet, his hands clinging to the top edge of the ramp. Slowly he moved his point of balance until he was standing on one hand! With the other, he reached inside his pocket and pulled something out. For a second, he held it up in the air.

"That's my phone!" I yelled.

Quick as a flash, the skater tossed the phone as high as he could. He let go of the edge of the ramp and skated back down to the bottom, just in time to pluck the phone out of the air before it hit the ground. By this point, everyone was watching—including the security guards, who'd caught on that something wasn't quite going as scheduled.

The skater pulled off his helmet and did a little bow. When he straightened up, I saw a telltale flash of blue hair in the sun.

Lenni!

She seemed to be looking right at me. She stuck her tongue out and waggled the phone. Then she hopped back on her board, skating her way through the crowd. Bystanders, still applauding, parted to let her through.

"Come on!" I yelled at Joe. "Now's our chance to catch her."

We took off running after her—and so did Tyrone's new security guards. They must have been briefed about her. Every single one of them was battling their way through the crowd. They looked like an army of linebackers, shoving people out of the way in their haste to catch up with Lenni.

Within seconds, the competition had turned into a stampede!

Over the River and Through the Woods

As soon as Lenni started off through the crowd, the entire skate park became a mad scene. Most people thought her little display was a halftime act for the Skate or Die Competition, or maybe even some sort of commercial stunt for a new brand of cell phone. But Tyrone must have alerted all his new security guards to be on the lookout for Lenni, and though they were slow, they weren't that stupid. There weren't that many amazing skater girls out there with short spiky blue hair.

The guards charged straight through the crowd, trying to get to Lenni. She must have ducked down low on her board, because I couldn't see her anywhere. The only sign of her was the motion of the crowd parting in front of her. But the guards made it impossible to follow that trail. They were like bulls running through the streets of Spain, and the crowd started running and dodging to get out of their way. People were pushing and shoving, being knocked to the ground.

A little kid, maybe ten or twelve, with short brown hair and a T-shirt with a picture of Cody Zane on it, was shoved to the ground directly in front of us. It looked like he was about to get trampled. He was so small, no one even noticed he was there. His screams could barely be heard over the noise of the crowd. Frank and I dived in. I pushed the crowd back while Frank lifted the kid up on his shoulders.

"Hey man, it's okay. I've got you," Frank said. "You here with someone?"

The kid was crying and nearly incoherent.

"We need to get him somewhere safe," I said. "Besides, there's no way we'll catch up with Lenni now. I can't see her through the crowd." The competition had become a wild mess, and the security guards Tyrone had been so excited about were making it worse by the second. I looked around for someplace safe, but everywhere was chaos. Then an idea came to me.

"Up here!" I yelled to Frank, pointing to the top of the ramp on which Lenni had been skating. The kid would be safe there from the crowd, and he would be visible, so anyone looking for him would have an easy time finding him.

I clambered up the side of the ramp and reached down to take the kid from Frank's hands.

"What's your name?" I asked him.

"Jamie," he said. He'd stopped crying now.

"Okay, Jamie, listen up. I need you to stay here until everything calms down. Got it?"

Jamie nodded, but he still looked scared.

"I'm a personal friend of Cody," I told him. "If you stay up here, I'll make sure you get to meet him later. Cool?"

"Yeah!" he shouted. "Cody's my hero!"

"Good deal," I said. I held up my hand, and Jamie slapped it five. Then he sat down, ready to wait out the mini-riot below for a chance to meet his idol.

"Are you here with anyone?" I asked Jamie.

"My mom," he said. "But we got separated when everyone started running."

"Do you have a cell phone?" Jamie nodded, and together we called his mom. She was nearly hysterical with worry, but we let her know where to find her son once the mayhem was under control.

I was about to hop back down when I realized something.

"Hey, Frank! Get up here."

Frank leaped up and grabbed the edge of the ramp. With one hand, I helped pull him up. From the top of the ramp, we could see the entire skating area. Maybe we hadn't lost our chance at catching Lenni yet.

"We might be able to spot Lenni, if she hasn't completely disappeared already."

For a long moment, Frank and I were silent, searching the edges of the crowd with our eyes.

"Whatcha doing?" Jamie asked.

"We're looking for someone," said Frank. "Want to help?"

"Sure!" Jamie said. "Who is it?"

"Well, did you see the girl who was skating here before? The one with blue hair?"

Jamie nodded.

"You mean her?" he asked, and pointed right beneath us.

Somehow Lenni had doubled back through the crowd and was standing on her board, right next to the ramp!

"You want this?" she yelled up, and flashed Frank's phone at him again. Then she kicked off and started making her way back through the crowd.

"Remember, stay here until your mom comes!" I yelled at Jamie. Then Frank and I jumped off the edge of the ramp and went after Lenni. Most of the crowd had cleared out of the area by this point, but we still had to dodge occasional passersby. Lenni used them as barriers. Every time we got close, she would put a person between us and her, making Frank and me slow down or stumble. Somehow she managed to stay just out of our reach. Like she was teasing us.

Most of the guards had already spread out to other parts of the park, looking for Lenni. But a few—either the slowest or the smartest—had stuck around. Soon there was a line of us: Lenni out in front on her skateboard, Frank and I right after her, and a bunch of security gorillas trailing behind us.

Lenni led us out of the skating area and away from the populated parts of the park. Some of the sections of Galaxy X weren't open to the public yet, and it was in this direction that Lenni headed.

"What's over this way?" I asked Frank as we ran along behind her.

"I think it's the Jungle!"

The Jungle, I remembered from looking at the Galaxy X brochure, was a giant wilderness obstacle course area. It would be tough to follow her in there, but she wouldn't be able to skate as easily, so we had a shot.

One by one, the security guards behind us dropped off, until only a dozen or so were still following. At the edge of the Jungle was a giant chasm, like a smaller version of the Grand Canyon, which separated it from the rest of the park. The only way across was by zip line. When this part of the park was up and functional, there would be attendants waiting to clip people into special harnesses, to make sure no one fell while crossing. Now there were just the long metal wires stretching out across the empty space. There were handles you could hold on to, but without the harnesses, one slip and you would fall all the way to the bottom of the chasm.

I thought we had her then, but Lenni didn't even slow down. When she reached the lip of the canyon, she leaped. One hand held her skateboard, the other grabbed one of the zip lines.

SSSSZZZZP!

She was all the way across before we even made it to the edge. There were only ten lines, total. Frank and I hopped on two of the remaining ones and sped after Lenni. Far behind, a few of the remaining guards took zip lines as well, but most had given up.

Finally we were officially in the Jungle. Tyrone had had the entire area landscaped to look like a tropical jungle. There were giant ferns all around, with small dirt paths running through them. It looked like something out of *Jurassic Park*. Lenni had a lead on us, but not much of one. We just had to figure out which way she'd gone.

"Do you hear anything?" I whispered to Frank.

He shook his head. Then he paused, put one finger to his lips, and pointed into the woods to our right. I cocked my head and listened. There was something moving quietly our way.

Quickly we worked our way over to the sides of the path. I crouched in the bushes on one side, while Frank did the same on the other. As soon as she walked out of the forest, we had her. The sound came closer and closer. I held up one hand and counted down.

Five . . . four . . . three . . . two . . . one . . .

We leaped—straight into the path of an oncoming tiger!

My heart jumped out of my chest and I froze. A scream rang out behind me. I looked back to see the first two guards to make it across the zip line fleeing in terror. The tiger stalked slowly toward us. Its head came up to my chest, and when it opened its muzzle, its teeth were as long as my fingers. Frank started laughing.

"Frank!" I hissed. "Be quiet." Our only chance was to stand as still as possible and hope it left us alone. No wonder this part of the park wasn't open to the public yet!

"Someone didn't read the Galaxy X brochure," said Frank as he reached out to pet the tiger. "They're robots. Animatronics. Totally harmless."

The tiger rubbed its head against Frank's hand, for all the world like a giant kitten. It purred deep in its chest. I could just make out the little blinking transmitter below its left ear.

I heard laughter coming from farther down the path.

"That's no robot," I said. Through the underbrush, I could see blue hair and a human form, rushing away.

We ran after her, but somehow Lenni was always just too far ahead for us to catch up. It almost seemed like she was toying with us. A suspicion began to grow in my mind, but just then we reached another obstacle—a long, flowing river. The only way to cross was a set of monkey bars that rose over the water. Again I thought we had her, but Lenni pulled herself up on top of the bars. She placed the wheels of her board on either side of one of the long beams and pushed off. She barely seemed to notice that she was skating on a thin bar, barely the width of her wheels, over a rushing river. She was that good.

Hand over hand, Frank and I hauled ourselves across the bars. Behind us, we heard a splashing sound and some cursing. I looked down in time to see the last two of the guards pulling themselves out of the river. Soaked and sullen, they sat on the bank. Clearly they were done chasing Lenni.

"So much for our replacements," said Frank, and laughed. Once we'd collared Lenni, I wondered how eager Tyrone would be to get rid of us.

On the other side of the river was a field of hurdles. Lenni was leaping over some and ducking under others. At one point, she even lay down on her board to get through some of them. The things she could do on a skateboard were amazing! I never stood a chance against her in the competition. Even Cody Zane himself would have a hard time keeping up with her.

Thankfully, ATAC had us run courses like this all the time. It was actually kind of fun. If we weren't chasing an incredibly athletic murderer through an empty jungle, I would have been having a great time.

"She can't go . . . much farther," Frank puffed between hurdles.

"I don't know. . . . Seems like . . . she could go all day," I panted. Lenni didn't seem to be tired at all.

"No. The park ends . . . up ahead. We've got her."

Frank was right. At the end of the obstacle course, the path turned sharply to the left. We ran for about another fifty feet before we burst out into a clearing. There was no other way in or out of the area aside from the trail we'd been running on.

There was also no sign of Lenni.

I felt a buzzing in my pocket, and then the first notes of "(No More) Mr. Nice Guyz" started playing.

"You have *that* as your ring tone?" Frank said in disbelief.

"It's catchy!" I protested as I pulled the phone out of my pocket. Then I saw who was calling and froze.

"Frank Hardy," the screen read.

FRANK

15

Can You Hear Me Now?

I took the phone out of Joe's hand. I looked around, but Lenni was nowhere in sight. After a moment, I answered it.

"Hello?"

"You're surrounded," Lenni's voice crackled through the receiver. "Put your hands up and I'll let you live."

The forest was silent around us. I tried to peer into the deep undergrowth, but I couldn't see anything. There might not have been a single other person in the Jungle. But then again, it was dark and overgrown enough that there could be a dozen people hiding out there. I strained my ears, hoping that even one or two of Tyrone's hired thugs had been able to catch up with us, but we were alone.

"Joe, put up your hands." I didn't want to get us killed, and for the moment, it seemed we had no choice but to play along with Lenni.

"What?"

I put my hands above my head, and after a second, Joe followed my example.

A laugh rang out over our heads. It had to be Lenni. Her laugh was instantly recognizable. It was low and gruff, like her voice, but joyful. It was the kind of laugh that made you want to laugh along with her. She was the most likable murderer I'd ever met. A skateboard fell out of a tree fifteen feet behind us. Joe nearly jumped out of his skin. A second later Lenni leaped down out of the tree and was standing on the board she had dropped, one foot poised to kick off and send her hurtling away.

I lowered my arms and looked at the distance between us. There was no way we could reach her before she skated off.

"You know, it's really hard to get the two of you alone. You make a girl work for it." Lenni smiled.

She was trying to get *us* alone? What the . . . ? Didn't she realize we'd been trying to arrest her? I took a step toward her, and she rolled back a few feet.

"Uh-uh," she said. "Not so fast. You're not getting

anywhere near me. Not just yet. I've got a few things to say first."

"Why did you bring us out here?" Joe asked, confused and impatient as to what was going on.

"I bet you're wondering why I brought you out here," said Lenni. Then she paused and laughed again. "Sorry, I've just always wanted to say that. Anyway. I know you think I killed Bret Johnston, but that's totally whack—I would never do anything like that. I mean, sure, his singing made me want to die, but that's no reason to kill him. Or at least, not enough reason."

"Sure," I said. "And all the protesting, the banner drop, and the flyers—those weren't you either, right?" Did she think we were stupid?

"No, yeah, that stuff totally was me." Lenni seemed almost proud of herself. "And Tyrone McKenzie deserved all of it, because this park is fake and so is he. All he cares about is money. But everything I did was peaceful—nobody got hurt. All that dangerous stuff, that wasn't me or any of my friends. The worst we did was some graffiti and broken windows, that kind of stuff."

"And you expect us to believe you . . . *why*?" Joe asked.

"I did go to a lot of effort to get you out here, you realize. I didn't need to do any of this. I grew up on this island! If I wanted to hide, the two of you—and Tyrone's army of idiots—would never have been able to find me."

She had a point. But I still didn't think she was innocent. This was some sort of elaborate setup.

"Then what were you doing in the rafters when Bret was murdered? Skating practice?" I asked.

Lenni stuck her tongue out at me.

"As if. I don't need practice. I could win this competition with one leg tied behind my back. These so-called skaters are a pretty sad lot. No offense." She gestured to Joe, who shrugged his shoulders and tried not to look hurt.

"I was up there that night arranging another banner drop. I was going to throw it down right as the concert began, to let all these kids know what a jerk Tyrone is. Then you two found me and I didn't get a chance to do it. When the lights went out and everything went crazy, I just ran. If you guys don't believe me, you can go up there and look. The banner is still there, above the stage."

"So that's it? You're not guilty because of some stupid sign you left up there?" Joe was still hurt over the "so-called skaters" comment, I could tell. He had a point, though. This was a pretty weak defense.

"Hey! That banner took six hours to make, and

I did a pretty good drawing of Tyrone on it, so shut up. But no, that's not all I had to tell you. I also found a really freaking important clue, but obviously you don't care."

Lenni started to skate off.

"Wait!" I yelled. What had she found?

She stopped and turned back, smiling.

"I was just kidding. Not about the clue—about leaving. I was there early, to set up the banner, right? Anyway, there was someone else there, skulking around the electricity box. They were pretty sneaky—I ran right into them before I noticed they were there. It was so dark, I couldn't make out who it was. But they dropped this."

Lenni tossed something into the clearing toward us. It was one of the VIP golden keys! Only ten or twenty people had those. This narrowed down our suspect list quite a bit. It also explained how whoever it was got close enough to the rides and events to pull off all their sabotage. With one of these, they would be able to go anywhere in the park, no questions asked.

I stepped forward to pick it up, and this time Lenni didn't skate away.

"I don't like Tyrone," she said. "But I don't think anyone deserves to die because he made some stupid park."

With that, she skated off into the jungle.

"Wait," I yelled. "What about my phone?"

Lenni laughed again.

"This?" She held out the phone. "I think I'll keep it. It might be good for us to stay in touch. Besides, who knows when I might need you guys to return the favor and help me?"

With that, she was gone.

"This is crazy!" Joe said. "Do you think we can trust her?"

"I don't know . . . but where else would she have gotten one of these?" I held the key up in the air and looked at it closely. It was definitely the real thing—it was heavy and smooth, just like the ones Joe and I had been given.

"If she's telling the truth, that means the killer has to be somebody we know. We both have keys, and Tyrone and Erica and Nick, Cody and London and David . . . ," Joe trailed off, trying to think who else might have keys.

"Bret had one, and the rest of the Nice Guyz too. There were a bunch of other celebrities around—we'll have to get a list of VIPs from Tyrone."

I heard a noise coming from behind us in the forest. I wondered if it was Lenni coming back, or maybe one of the security guards finally catching up with us. I turned, but it was just one of the robot tigers. It emerged from the underbrush and started walking toward us. Then another appeared behind it, and then a third. Something about the way they were coming at us seemed . . . *wrong*.

"Frank?"

"Yeah?"

"Is it just me, or is something up with their programming?"

The three tigers had spread out and were now in a triangle pattern. They looked exactly like three real tigers—three real tigers hunting prey! One of the tigers threw back its head and roared.

"Watch out!" yelled Joe. The tiger in front leaned back on its haunches and leaped at us. We both dived to the side—right into the path of the other tigers! Joe managed to duck beneath the one that came at him, but the second tiger slammed straight into me, sending me flying through the air. Its huge jaws barely missed taking a chunk out of my arm.

"Someone's reprogrammed them!" I shouted.

"Thanks, Frank," Joe said, as the first tiger swiped at him again, its paw nearly as big as his head. "I hadn't noticed."

For the next few minutes, there were claws and fur flying everywhere. The three giant cats toyed with us like . . . cats with mice. One of the tigers backed me up against a tree. Its tail was twitching, and I could tell it was just waiting for the right moment to pounce on me. I watched its eyes, waiting, waiting, waiting . . . then it jumped right at me!

There were trees to either side of me and nowhere to go, so I leaped straight up. I grabbed a branch above my head and pulled my body up into the trees. The robot tiger slammed straight into the trunk of the tree below me. The little receiver below its ear crumpled on impact. The tiger fell to the ground and didn't get back up again.

"The receiver! Joe, hit them in the receiver!" That was the only way to stop them.

I looked over to see if Joe had heard me, only to find the two other tigers had him cornered. One reached out and batted at him. Joe dodged out of the way, and the other tiger took a swipe that sent him to the ground. As one, the two tigers prepared to pounce on him.

I dropped out of the tree and raced toward him, but there was no way I was going to get there in time. Joe grabbed the first of the tigers by its neck. He'd managed to pick up a rock off the ground, and he was pushing its jaws away with one hand while his other smashed the rock against it, trying blindly to find the receiver.

The other tiger came up behind him. It reared up onto its hind legs, its powerful front paws getting ready to rip his head right off. I was too far away to do anything.

Out of the trees, something came hurtling end over end, smashing the tiger in the side of the head. Its receiver exploded in a puff of smoke and blue light. At the same time, Joe finally smashed the receiver on the one he was wrestling. Both tigers fell to the ground. Without their programming, they were just lifeless hunks of metal.

Lenni strolled back into the clearing.

"You know, you guys should really be more careful. This place is pretty dangerous these days, and I can't always be around to look out for you."

With that, she picked up her skateboard from underneath the tiger she had hit with it and skated off down the path. Joe and I sat in silence for a second, the only sound our own heavy breathing.

"You know," Joe said after a moment of staring at the deactivated tiger that had been about to decapitate him before Lenni broke it, "she's pretty cute."

Video Games Killed the Skateboard Star

"Can't believe she stole your phone, man. I mean, that's just sad." Frank was so organized, I rarely got the chance to tease him for losing stuff, so I was going to make the most of this opportunity.

He ignored me and continued walking. We were almost back to the Skate or Die Competition area, having safely made it out of the Jungle without any more animal incidents. We'd disabled the zip lines so no one else could get in until we could warn Tyrone about the reprogrammed robots. Lenni, we figured, would be able to get out on her own. She could handle herself.

"Not only did she take it from you once, but she

got away with it *again*. That's like losing it twice. Three times, if you count the time she came back when the tigers attacked."

"You mean, when she came back to save *you* from those tigers? And she may have taken my phone, but at least she didn't completely destroy me during the skating competition."

"Sorry, I can't hear you—I'm on my phone." I was dialing Tyone to let him know what had gone down. Perhaps now that his security guards had totally failed him, he wouldn't be so eager to let us go.

"Talk."

That was all his voice mail said. I told him it was urgent that he call me—not Frank, because *he'd* lost his phone. Frank shot me a dirty look.

"Come on," he said. "Let's go find out if Lenni was telling the truth."

We swung by the competition area first, just to make sure no damage had been done by the guards. It was calm now, and it looked as though the guard stampede hadn't done any major damage. Results from day two of the competition were posted, listing the top five skaters who would appear in the finale tomorrow. I was glad to see Rose's name among them. After a casual look around the place, we headed over to the stage where the Blastoff had been.

"Uh-oh," Frank said. He stopped.

"What's the problem?"

"We're not on the case anymore, remember?" He pointed. The stage area was covered in caution tape and surrounded by guards. "I doubt they're going to just let us in."

"Lenni found a way in. If she can do it, we can." I looked up at the stage. There had to be a way. Then I spotted it. "Follow me," I told Frank.

We walked the long way around the stage, careful to stay out of sight of the guards. When Frank realized where we were headed, he paused.

"I don't need to use the restroom." There was a long row of porta-potties ahead of us.

"Those are our ticket to the stage. Boost me up."

Frank made a cradle with his hands and I stepped into it.

"One, two . . . three!" On the count of three, I jumped up and Frank lifted with all his might, sending me flying through the air. I landed safely on top of the porta-potty. I leaned down and gave him a hand up. We were now at the back of the stage area, and from here it was just possible to leap up and grab the edge of the beams that held up the wiring and lights. This must have been how Lenni got up unseen.

From there, it was easy to climb up the scaffolding and into the ceiling of the stage. No one could see you up here, even in the daylight. Frank and I split up and searched the beams for the banner.

"Found it!" Frank whispered loudly, after only a few minutes. The banner was huge, probably thirty feet by ten feet, and it had a drawing of Tyrone, complete with devil horns and a tail on one side. There was an image of Cody as well, and in between were the words SOLD OUT? OR SELL-OUT?

"That's a pretty good likeness," I said.

"Yeah," Frank agreed. "But it doesn't prove she's innocent. She could have put this up here any time."

"But she had the key—where else could she have gotten it?"

"True. We need to find out who Tyrone gave these keys to, and whose is missing."

"It's only VIPs, right?"

Frank nodded.

"Well," I continued, "all the VIPs who haven't left already should be at the PowerUp Play-Off tonight."

To celebrate the finale of the competition, Tyrone and Cody were hosting a Skate or Die video game party at the Videodrome, the Galaxy X arcade.

PowerUp, the official energy drink of Cody Zane and the Zaniacs, was sponsoring it. Any celebrities who hadn't taken off running should be there— and I had no doubt Lenni and her friends would probably put in an appearance as well. It was our last best chance to figure this case out.

We took the banner down from the stage area and carefully snuck it out the back with us. Depending on what we found out tonight, it was either evidence that Lenni was innocent, or further proof that she had been involved with all the troubles plaguing the park. We hid it in our room and got ready, making sure we had our own VIP keys with us in order to get us into the Videodrome.

Like everything else at Galaxy X, the Videodrome was over the top. It was a giant sphere made of special glass, wired to broadcast the images from the video games being played inside. The pictures moved and shifted. At first, one video game would appear fifty feet tall along the entire side of the building, and then it would break apart into a dozen smaller pictures. It was almost as fun to watch the games as it was to play.

Galaxy X may have emptied out a little after the last few accidents, but with every person left packed into the Videodrome, it was a madhouse. There must have been a thousand people, easily, playing every video game imaginable. There were first-person shooters, games where you wore virtual reality helmets, games with joysticks, guns, special pads that recorded your every movement. There were racing games with cars built to look like the actual cars in the games, flight simulators built to look like jet fighters, and even one game where players climbed inside submarines that were lowered into a giant aquarium.

The biggest attraction, however, was the Head-2-Head Arena. Here two players could battle it out in one game, which was broadcast on two giant television screens that floated at the very center of the Videodrome. The winner would receive a lifetime supply of PowerUp, as well as free passes to come back to Galaxy X anytime.

There was music and noise all around us. Flashing lights, people running, yelling, cheering—it was total chaos. And totally awesome!

"Would you like a free PowerUp, the official beverage of the Cody Zane Skate or Die Competition?" A beautiful blond woman dressed in the PowerUp colors—bright red and electric yellow—offered us a tray of drinks.

"Thanks," I said. "I've never had a PowerUp before."

"It's delicious!" she replied. I noticed she was hiding a bottle of water in her pocket.

"Then why aren't you drinking one?" I asked.

"Uh, well. That's a good question, but I have to go work the front door now. Have a great competition!"

With that, she ran off.

"This place is a nightmare," said Frank.

"More like a dream come true! Look, they have ZOMG Kill 4! That hasn't even been released yet!" ZOMG 3 was my favorite video game ever, hands down. It was like an ATAC mission—with zombies. Zombies make everything cooler. Maybe once we made sure Cody was safe, I could come back and check the game for clues. . . .

"There are so many fake guns and so much screaming here, if anyone tried to hurt Cody, we'd never even notice."

Frank really knew how to bring the fun. But he had a point. It was a pretty dangerous place. Luckily, the VIP area was kept separate from everything else. It was a special glass cube at the center of the Videodrome, on a platform right below the screens that broadcast the games in the Head-2-Head Arena. Everyone could see it, but no one could see into it, because the glass was one way only. It should have been pretty safe, but I wasn't taking anything for granted.

We flashed our keys to the guards at the stairs

leading up, and made our way to the lounge where Cody, David, Tyrone, Erica, and Nick were hanging out. Once inside the VIP area, the noise died down. The glass must have been soundproofed somehow. Some of Cody's entourage was there as well, but most of them seemed to have left with London. David seemed his usual surly self, but Cody was smiling. Everyone was holding a PowerUp, but no one seemed to be drinking them.

Frank went straight to Tyrone to explain everything we'd learned from Lenni. I could see Erica drifting closer to listen in. She had *such* a crush on Frank. She was always trying to be near him. Lucky Frank.

I sat down with David, Cody, and Nick.

"This stuff is disgusting," Nick said as I came over, pointing to the can of PowerUp he was holding.

"Yeah," I said. "So what's the deal with PowerUp, anyway?" I asked Cody. "You love it that much?"

"Well, actually . . ." Cody paused and looked around to see who was nearby, then dropped his voice to a whisper. "It's kind of gross," he said. "But they pay me a lot of money to drink it. Usually I just pour it out and refill the can with colored water."

Nick laughed. "No wonder you and my dad get along so well. You're both fake."

I couldn't believe Cody would spend all his time selling something he hated. That seemed way grosser than PowerUp could ever be. I didn't know what to say.

David sat up in a huff.

"I'm going to go play some games," he said, and stalked off before Cody or I could say anything.

"So that nut job didn't have anything to do with the disaster at my concert?" Tyrone burst in on us. Apparently, Frank had managed to give him the important details at least.

"No," I said. "And Lenni didn't kill Bret, either."

"Then who did?" Erica asked.

We didn't have an answer to that question yet, so I changed the subject.

"So we're back on the case?" I asked, enjoying making Tyrone admit he was wrong.

"What are you talking about? Hello! That's what I hired you for, remember? Just make sure nothing happens at the competition finale tomorrow. Erica, Nick—it's time to go. You both have to look fresh and happy for the press photos in the morning."

Apparently, Tyrone didn't remember firing us—or he wasn't going to admit it if he did. Erica and

Nick followed Tyrone sullenly out of the VIP area, and Frank and I were left alone with Cody and a few bodyguards.

"Hey, guys," Cody said to his guards. "Go play some games. Have some fun. Joe and Frank are here, and there are guards on the stairs leading up to the VIP area. Nothing's going to happen."

The guards were reluctant to leave, but when Cody gave them each a hundred-dollar bill to play games with, they went running.

"You guys want to play something?"

Cody pointed to the video game console at the center of the VIP area. It was like a smaller version of the Head-2-Head Arena, two screens floating in the middle of the room.

"Any game in the entire Videodrome can be played on these screens," Cody continued.

"Even ZOMG Kill 4?" I asked.

"ZOMG is, like, one of my favorite games of all time, man," Cody said.

"Mine too!"

"Excellent. Let's play!"

"You're on," I replied, and we high-fived.

Frank just rolled his eyes. Cody walked over toward the video screens. As he bent down to the control box underneath, I heard a sharp cracking sound. I looked around the VIP area, but I couldn't see anything that could have caused the noise. A sudden motion above Cody's head caught my attention. The screens! They were tipping forward and falling from the ceiling. Cody was so caught up in trying to get ZOMG Kill 4 running that he hadn't even noticed. In a second, he would be crushed beneath their weight.

Game Over

At the last minute, Cody realized something was wrong. He looked up at the giant screens slowly descending upon him. He froze in shock. As one, Joe and I ran forward and tackled him. It was so close, I could feel the rush of air as the screens smashed to the ground behind us.

The crash was still ringing in my ears as Cody, Joe, and I sat up. There were shards of glass all over us, and Cody had a cut across his forehead, but no one seemed seriously injured.

"Are you okay?" Joe said, turning to Cody.

Cody nodded, too stunned to speak.

Though the cube was soundproofed, the crash was so loud, the guards at the bottom of the stairs must have heard something. A pair of them came running up together. They stopped at the entrance to the room, clubs drawn. There was glass everywhere, and sparks flying from the wreckage of the video screens. They seemed unsure what to do.

"You!" I said, pointing to one of the guards. "Go get the power turned off before those sparks start a fire."

The guard hesitated for a second, weighing the danger of leaving his post and getting in trouble with Tyrone against the danger of being the one responsible for a fire in the VIP section. Then he took off running.

"This is . . . this is just too much," Cody mumbled under his breath.

"You sure you're all right?" Joe asked him, reaching over to wipe the blood off Cody's face.

"All right? ALL RIGHT?" Cody's calm finally cracked. "No, I'm not all right. In case you haven't noticed, someone is trying to kill me! This whole place is cursed. I should have listened to London and gotten out of here days ago."

He was screaming now, almost as loud as Tyrone. "I'm getting out of here. Tonight."

Cody stood up and pulled out his cell phone. "David?"

He paused, listening. Then he frowned.

"Yeah, I'm all right. Did you hear the crash or something?" Before David could respond, he continued. "Look, get back to the VIP area. We're leaving tonight. As far as I'm concerned, this competition is over."

Joe's jaw dropped. Cody snapped his phone shut and began picking pieces of glass out of his clothes and throwing them angrily on the floor. I took Joe's phone from him and called Tyrone. I explained what had happened. He was yelling before I'd even finished with the story.

"That's not all," I told him. "Cody says he's leaving tonight."

Tyrone grew quiet, which was even scarier than his yelling.

"Keep him there," he said. "Just for fifteen minutes. I'm on my way. Don't let him leave. Do whatever it takes."

Short of tying him to one of the couches, I didn't think there was anything I could do to keep Cody at Galaxy X. I couldn't really blame him. If he hadn't believed it before, tonight had made it clear: Someone was out to get him, and they weren't going to stop until he was dead, or gone from Galaxy X. Maybe getting out of here would be the best thing for him.

There was a commotion down at the base of the steps.

What now? I thought. Could anything else go wrong tonight?

Joe and I ran carefully over to the top of the steps, avoiding the glass and the smoking wires. Behind us, Cody continued hurling pieces of the screen and talking to himself. I could hear David's voice coming from down below.

"I said let me in, you idiots! Get out of my way."

Before we could walk down the steps to investigate, Cody came over.

"This is ridiculous," he said. "The guards here can't stop someone from trying to kill me, but they can hassle my best friend endlessly. All because he lost that stupid key Tyrone gave him."

Something clicked in my mind.

"He lost what?" asked Joe. I could see by the expression on his face that he was thinking the same thing I was.

"His VIP pass. During the chaos at the concert he must have dropped it, and someone probably took it as a souvenir. I've had to vouch for him everywhere we go since then."

I looked at Joe. He nodded.

"Stay here," I said to Cody. "No matter what you do. Don't leave this room, and don't let anyone in except for us or Tyrone. Got it?"

"No way, man, I'm getting out of here as soon as David—"

"Don't even let David in," Joe cut him off. "Especially not David."

Cody looked like he was going to argue with Joe.

"Trust me," Joe said. Cody nodded.

We raced down the steps two at a time. David was still arguing with the guards at the bottom.

"What's going on?" I asked.

"These morons won't let me in." David seemed to have only one emotion: whiny. And I'd thought Bret Johnston was bad. David was ten times worse.

"Oh," I said, playing dumb. "Just show them your key."

"If it was that easy, I'd be in the VIP area already." He looked at me as though I was an idiot. "I can't find the stupid thing."

"Really?" said Joe. "Because Frank and I found this one over on the stage after the concert the other night."

Joe pulled the key Lenni had given us out of his pocket. David snatched for it, but Joe pulled it just out of reach.

"Give that back to me!" David said. His voice was high and shaky. He was nervous.

"Not so fast," I said. "What were you doing over by the electrical box?"

"That's easy to explain," David said. "I was—"

Suddenly David shoved Joe and sent him flying into me. We stumbled backward as he took off running into the Videodrome. The guards were too shocked to do anything.

"What are you guys doing?" Cody's voice came from behind us. Looks like he hadn't listened to Joe after all.

"Stay here!" I yelled. Then Joe and I ran off after David.

I could just make out his black-and-white-striped shirt disappearing down one of the long rows of arcade games. We raced after him. David ran straight into people, knocking them over left and right. As we ran, we had to jump and dodge around the people he left sprawled in his wake. I heard the loud footsteps of someone following us, and turned around to see Cody right on our tail.

Joe was slightly ahead of me as we came to the end of the row of games. As he stopped to look and see which way David had gone, there came a low rumbling sound.

"Look out!" I yelled. Joe jumped out of the way just as one of the arcade games came crashing down right where he had been standing. There was a puff of smoke from the inside of the machine, and I could smell plastic burning. We climbed over it and continued after David.

Occasionally I lost sight of David as we ran, but it was easy to track the chaos he left behind him: people screaming, games knocked over. Even in the general noise and crowd of the Videodrome, he was obvious.

He ran toward the section of old-fashioned games: pinball, skee-ball, air hockey. Once he ducked through the doors, he was out of sight. Luckily, the area was a dead end. We got inside, then paused for a moment, looking for him. But he was nowhere to be seen.

"Ooph!"

Something heavy had hit me in the chest, and I staggered to one side. A skee-ball bounced on the ground in front of me. Another came whizzing at Joe's head, missing him by only a few short inches. We ducked and wove our way forward to the corner where the balls were coming from.

"You're not getting out of here, David," I yelled. "Tyrone's security guards are at every door. You might as well give yourself up."

I had learned something from Lenni. Tyrone had fired all his new security people and probably didn't have enough to stop David from getting out of here if he managed to avoid us—but he didn't know that.

The balls stopped flying. David was nowhere in sight. This area of the Videodrome was slightly quieter than the rest, perhaps because many of the games were old-fashioned hand games and carnival games, without electronics or speakers.

"There!" Cody whispered, pointing up toward the basket of a beanbag toss game. I could just make out a tuft of spiky black hair jutting up over the rim.

I gestured to Cody to be quiet. Joe and I climbed up either side of the basket. On the count of three, we reached down and grabbed David by the arms, yanking him out of his hiding place.

He came out passively. The energy seemed to have gone right out of him once he realized he was caught—until he saw Cody. Suddenly he was screaming and thrashing. He yanked his arm free of my grip. With his now free hand, he shoved Joe backward as hard as he could. Joe stumbled to the ground but managed to pull David down with him. I leaped on top of them, and between us, Joe and I pinned him to the ground.

"This is your fault!" David screamed at Cody. "You forgot about me—you forgot about skating. All you care about is money and sponsorships and being famous! And they all eat it up." His voice went high and wispy, like a girl's. "*Oh Cody, we love you*. It makes me sick."

Cody's face went white. His mouth was moving, but nothing came out. Finally, after a minute, he managed to speak.

"But . . . I thought you were my friend," he said.

David continued to scream at him until Tyrone showed up a few minutes later with the police in tow. Apparently, dozens of people had called security to report David running wild through the Videodrome, and Tyrone had thought to bring actual police this time.

We handed David's key over to the officers and explained everything that Lenni had told us previously, although we left out the banner she had been intending to drop at the concert and her breaking and entering.

David was done yelling now. He seemed defeated, and in an almost normal tone of voice, he told the cops all of it. How he had started off just wanting to make Tyrone cancel the competition, by sending him threatening text messages as "4Real." When that didn't work, he tried to injure Cody, to make him pull out of participating. When Joe got hurt on the ramp instead, and Cody continued to ignore him, David went further and further, finally trying to electrocute Cody on the night of the concert.

"What about the tigers?" I asked. "And the rides you broke—you could have hurt a lot of other people."

David looked confused.

"I don't know what you're talking about," he said. "I didn't touch the rides. I thought they just broke. And I've never even seen a tiger up close."

He also claimed to have no idea who Sk8rH8r was. As the cops pulled him to his feet and cuffed his hands behind him, I felt a chill in the pit of my stomach, but I tried to wave it away. He was probably just lying to save himself from a longer time in jail . . . I hoped.

I almost felt sorry for him. It must have been hard to be less famous than Cody, and feel like he was losing his friendship. But losing a friend didn't justify murder.

18

An Explosive Performance

'll give Tyrone this: He was a smart business-
man. Before the cops had even hauled David
Sanders out of the Videodrome, he was on the
phone with every major TV station and newspaper,
spreading the story that the "plot against Cody
Zane" had been foiled by the "special undercover
agents" Tyrone had hired—aka Frank and me.
Thankfully, he didn't mention us by name, but
our cover here was definitely blown.

By the next morning, the crowds had returned
to Galaxy X three times as large. London was back
at the judges' table, freshly tanned from her modeling shoot. Everyone was in a great mood—Tyrone
actually hugged Frank! Even the small legion of

girls who had begun to build a memorial to Bret Johnston seemed slightly happier today, or at least less afraid that they were going to get blown up.

After David was arrested, Cody decided to stick around Galaxy X. He seemed pretty shaken by all the things David had said about him, but I think it made him all the more determined to stay for the rest of the competition. There were only five skaters left, and today one of them would be crowned the winner of the Cody Zane Skate or Die Competition. Since we were back in Tyrone's good graces, he had invited us to sit up at the judges' table, but Frank and I decided to keep a low profile and stay in the crowd. No pointing in making it obvious who Tyrone's two "secret agents" were. Now we were just waiting for the event to start.

"Hey, guys."

A voice from behind me in the crowd startled me out of my thoughts. I turned around, and there was Lenni with a wide grin on her face. She had a long blond wig on and was wearing a dress and sandals. I almost didn't recognize her. I had to admit, I was surprised to see her hanging out at Galaxy X, given her hatred for the place.

"Hey!" said Frank. "You might not want to be here. I think Tyrone is still pretty angry at you."

"Why, thank you, Frank. Yes, I did break this case wide open for you. You are so welcome," Lenni declared, in a tone of fake sincerity. Frank blushed and stammered an apology. I rushed in to save him.

"He just doesn't want to see anything happen to you, after you rescued us and everything."

"Hello!" Lenni pointed to the outfit she was wearing. "I can play secret agent too, you know?"

She turned away from us for a second to hand some flyers to two guys walking past. "Galaxy X is a land-stealing corporation. All they care about is your money. Check out the truth. Have a good day!" The guys seemed confused, but when Lenni smiled at them, they took the pieces of paper from her and wandered off.

"Works every time," she said.

I was glad to see she hadn't changed her tune. She might have been a bit of a loose cannon, but she stuck to her principles. I respected her for that. I just hoped that she really wasn't involved in any of the serious trouble happening at Galaxy X. Even though we had David Sanders in custody, there were still some accidents left unexplained. I hated to think she could be behind them . . . but I wanted to keep tabs on her anyway.

"Are you going to stick around for the end of the

competition?" I asked. "You know, you deserve to be up there."

"I'll be around. But really, I shouldn't be up there." She paused, then smiled again. "I'm better than they are."

Frank laughed, and Lenni wandered off into the crowd, handing out more flyers as she went.

"Somehow," he said, "I don't think that's the last we're going to see of her."

"Yeah. I just hope we're on the same side next time."

The rest of the competition went smoothly. Each of the five skaters was given fifteen minutes to show off. Since the prize was to have a character created in your image in the upcoming video game, the skaters tried to show off their personality as well as their skills on the board.

Rose was definitely the crowd favorite. She must have had friends in the audience, because when her turn came, the crowd pelted the area around the judges' table with hundreds of roses in all different colors. The press loved it, snapping pictures and shooting video left and right, which made Tyrone even happier. This was the kind of headline he wanted to make. Cody had a huge grin on his face, and when Rose finished skating, he picked up one of the flowers off the stage and handed it to her. London looked a little bit irritated at that, but she laughed along with everyone else.

It was no surprise when Rose was announced the winner of the tournament. After he called her name, Cody motioned for the crowd to be quiet.

"I want to thank you all," he said. "This competition was tough, and though there can be only one winner, I've seen a hundred amazing skaters over the past three days. More than that, I've seen the love of skating that everyone in this crowd has. I'd forgotten that part of skating, I think. When you become famous at something, it stops being about the love, and it all gets caught up in the money or the reputation. But today, everyone is here for the love. Which is why I'm going to do something I haven't done in a long time."

Cody took a step back from the podium and walked over to the judges' table. He lifted his Hubris brand skateboard over his shoulder and smashed the glass that protected his famous first skateboard. The crowd realized what was about to happen and went wild. Cody lifted the board out of the wreckage of the glass, strapped on his helmet, and walked down to the skating ramp.

"Cody, Cody, Cody!"

The crowd was chanting his name as he prepared

to skate. He kicked off the side of the ramp and flew down toward the middle.

But something was wrong. He was wobbling on the board. As he tried to do a jump, the board flew out from under him. Cody's head slammed into the side of the ramp, and he went down hard.

The stunned crowd stood in a shocked silence. Frank and I ran over to the ramp. Frank knelt by Cody's body.

"He's still breathing. Someone call an ambulance!" he shouted.

There was a wave of beeps and blips as hundreds of cell phones all dialed 911 at the same time. I grabbed Cody's skateboard to make sure it didn't get lost. It felt strangely heavy, and there was an odd sound coming from it. I flipped it over.

"Frank!"

I showed the back of the skateboard to him. Strapped to the bottom was a black box with a digital counter on it. It was a bomb—and it was wired to go off in fifteen seconds!

"Get Cody out of here!" I yelled to Frank.

The counter on the bomb clicked down. Fourteen seconds. Thirteen. Twelve. Eleven.

Cody started to wake up, but he was too disoriented to move. I looked around frantically. The crowd surrounded us a hundred feet in every direction. There was no way to get the bomb to some safe, empty place before it blew.

Suddenly Lenni came flying out of the crowd. She grabbed the board from my hands.

"What are you doing?" I screamed. This was suicide.

Lenni ignored me and began skating. She went up one side of the ramp and down the other, gaining speed with each pass. I knew the timer was ticking down on the bottom of the board, and under my breath I counted down the seconds.

Five . . . four . . . three . . .

Lenni was skating as fast as I had ever seen anyone go. She made it to the top of the ramp with one second left on the timer. Right at the peak, she leaped off the boards. Free of Lenni's weight, the skateboard continued on its way, flying off the top edge of the ramp and straight up into the air. Just as Lenni landed back down at the bottom of the ramp, it exploded harmlessly in the air.

The crowd, still confused as to what was happening, looked over at Cody. Frank had managed to get him on his feet, but the noise of the bomb startled him, and he slipped. From a distance, it looked as though he had bowed.

From the judges' table, Tyrone's voice boomed out over the microphone.

"That was one explosive performance, eh? Let's have a round of applause for Cody Zane and Lenni Wolff!" Tyrone was probably furious, but he did a good job of hiding it. He made it sound like the explosion was on purpose, and the crowd believed him. As one, they began chanting Lenni's name.

No way, I thought. *She beat me again!*